The Country Road

The Country Road
Stories

Regina Ullmann

Translated from the German by Kurt Beals

A NEW DIRECTIONS PAPERBOOK

Copyright © 2007 by Nagel & Kimche im Carl Hanser Verlag
Translation copyright © 2015 by Kurt Beals

Originally published as *Die Landstrasse* in 1921.

TRANSLATOR'S NOTE: I would like to thank all of the organizations and individuals who
have supported this translation and made its publication possible. I am especially grateful
to the Banff International Literary Translation Centre (BILTC) at the Banff Centre, Alberta,
Canada, and my colleagues there who provided feedback and insights about early
drafts of the translation, as well as to the Kulturförderung Kanton Wallis, which allowed me to spend three months in the Übersetzungsatelier Raron in the Swiss Alps
completing this translation. In addition, I was delighted and honored to receive a grant from
the PEN/Heim Translation Fund, and I greatly appreciate the judges' confidence in this work.
    This translation received additional support from the Max Geilinger-Stiftung, the
Regina-Ullmann-Fonds of the Kantonsbibliothek Vadiana St. Gallen, and the Kulturförderung Kanton St. Gallen, and I am grateful to all of these organizations for helping to bring
this long-neglected Swiss author to the attention of a broader international audience.
    In addition, I would like to thank the friends and colleagues who helped me unravel
some of Ullmann's most difficult passages, particularly Anja Beuthe, who provided valuable feedback at many points.

Manufactured in the United States of America
New Directions Books are printed on acid-free paper.
First published as New Directions Paperbook 1298 in 2015.
Design by Erik Rieselbach

Library of Congress Cataloging-in-Publication Data
Ullmann, Regina, 1884–1961
[Landstrasse. English]
The country road : stories / Regina Ullmann ; translated from the German by Kurt Beals.
— First edition.
pages cm
ISBN 978-0-8112-2005-7 (alk. paper)
1. Ullmann, Regina, 1884–1961—Translations into English. I. Beals, Kurt. II. Title.
PT2643.L53L2613 2015
833'.912—dc23   2014027198

10 9 8 7 6 5 4 3 2 1

New Directions Books are published for James Laughlin
by New Directions Publishing Corporation
80 Eighth Avenue, New York 10011

Reverently dedicated to Ellen Delp

Contents

The Country Road

The Country Road

Part One

Summer, but a younger summer than this one; the summer back then was no more than my equal in years. True, I still wasn't happy, not happy to my core, but I had to be in the way that everyone is. The sun set me ablaze. It grazed on the green knoll where I sat, a knoll with an almost sacred form, where I had taken refuge from the dust of the country road. Because I was weary. I was weary because I was alone. This long country road before and behind me … The bends that it made around this knoll, the poplars—even heaven itself could not relieve it of its bleakness. I was ill at ease, because just a short way into my walk, this road had already dragged me into its misery and squalor. It was an uncanny country road. An all-knowing road. A road reserved for those who had been, in some way, left alone.

I, for my part, unpacked my provisions from my small satchel. The heat had rendered them inedible. I had to throw them away. Not even birds would have wanted them now. So in addition to everything else, this sense of deprivation left me hungry and thirsty. And there was no spring in sight. The knoll alone seemed to conceal the secret of a spring deep within it, beyond my reach. And even if I could have hoped to find a spring nearby, I still wouldn't have tried to reach it. I was tired and dry of tears, but close to crying.

Where were the pictures that had led me so blessedly through my childhood? They seemed to resemble this knoll. But then again, they didn't, because I was sitting there now. And I didn't belong in the picture anymore. I conjured up another; for the truth, which I did not spare myself, had given me a beggar's stubborn stance toward life. I wanted to have an ideal, an ideal (since the earlier ones were already taken from me) suited to my own being. And I recalled a painting by the young Raphael that depicted the dream of a youth. I had always found the purity of that image refreshing. Even today. But such purity was no longer my own. This image from my childhood seemed to grow on the knoll, and it drove me down, down to the dusty country road. But I was not yet fully exhausted.

Then in my mind Saint Anne's enormous bed arched up here on the hillside. An angel was holding the canopy's highest billow aloft in the clouds. Beneath it were women, many of them, all lovingly at work. They were bathing a newborn child, Mary. Here they carried in jugs, there they held linens at the ready. The picture was all love and joy, the purest joy on earth. I averted my eyes. Mechanically I looked down at the country road. None of that was really around me. I was alone on the knoll, cast out of myself, so to speak. This sensation is unknown to anyone who feels at home in bush and tree, who finds there a bed, a chest, a trestle; who finds a bouquet awaiting him at every stage of life. It is meant for him. Was it God, was it the father, the younger brother, who held it in his hand from the beginning?

My shoes were dusty, pinching from the heat. My dress had no need to please anyone on earth. Perhaps in the beginning it had had such a purpose, but that had been all too quickly forgotten. One must be reminded of such things. Whether it be the fish in the water or a birdsong or love, as only nature knows it—something must have reminded us of it. But I had already slipped my own mind.

Down below, weary merchant women were passing. In a moment they were all around, and then they had passed me by like a crescent moon. Next a herd came by, enveloped in its own dust like a cloud. A couple of children followed, holding empty baskets in their blue hands. They had a guilty conscience. From above, it was clear that they had stilled their hunger with the meager yield of their blueberry harvest. That was money that they had swallowed. They did not share in the happiness of those mountain children who once returned home from seeking berries to eat their pan of porridge, still spooning out their joy ...

I paused at this memory, my eyes still fixed on the road. An organ grinder passed, old, country road ... The silent organ hung on his back. A little dog ran after him, so close on his heels that it seemed to run underneath him, the way dogs run under a wagon's wheels when it's all they have to guard.

A fisherman passed—there was a man-made pond nearby.

Finally, along came a hideous bicyclist. He was a perfectly ordinary man. I could just clearly see the red handkerchief blowing from his breast pocket. Oh, how unhappy I was about this strange cyclist. Not even if the love of mankind had reconciled me to him, forcing me to reconsider, not even then would I have been able to smile again. And wasn't he laughable, this cyclist? Had I slowly lost all my gaiety in life, all my confidence?

With my hand I had idly plucked a woodruff. So it was May, then. Not July or August, not the hottest day of the year? Up above the country road I had lost all track of time. I held the blossom like an oracle. Then I laid it in my lap. I let out a gentle breath. Or it might have been a sigh.

The landscape around me was not beautiful. No, it was the melancholy landscape of a woeful country road, which never forgot for a moment that this dust was the debt it owed to itself, ankle-deep dust, ground fine by the millstones of the sun and the rising full moon.

A darkening, uncooled night, a day like today, like the glaze of the finest malachite, had ground it down for us, this dust that seemed to be everywhere. It was as if grandfather had left it for us, as he did for the serpent in paradise, this dust, the premature snow of old age coating the trees.

"Oh God!" This cry for help passed over my lips again and again, uncomprehended. I had not encountered it in a long time, this word. Truly, I no longer remembered it.

And you must encounter God in your own flesh.

Of course I knew that God's name was engraved in every animal. Every blade of grass bore his sharp inscription. Even the flowers held him in their curves. And what was their fragrance but yet another living thing from the hand of creation. I claimed to have no God. But there I was once again, holding the woodruff blossom in my hand. I was touched by the goodness that this blossom exhaled. I fell silent and watched.

Down below, on the country road, a horse and wagon were waiting in front of a low building. I had hardly noticed the building. Lost in thought, I had overlooked the horse and wagon. The horse stood under a chestnut tree and waited. He nibbled at the leaves, pulling the hay wagon behind him. A voice called for him to stop. That was all. Above the building hung a sign that bore the name: "The Sun Inn." I couldn't read it, but there was a picture, too. I stood up. It had occurred to me that this wagon could take me along for part of the way. Then at least I would be somewhere else. I headed down. I felt heavy, as if I were bearing burdens, unknown ones from all over the world. But it was only my own presence playing tricks on me. Presence: all at once I understood that worn-out word. It was well-suited to the country road.

I picked up my belongings from the ground. I took one last look at the world. Wasn't it beautiful, then?

Somewhere a child was wailing miserably, like the very young who seem to have no eyes. That was just what this country road had needed.

I stood beside the road below and waited. The horse approached in a circus trot, as if the world were a carousel that never came round to its end.

The man on the front bench—it wasn't a true box seat— was lenient with his whip. He was a young man. He shared the bench with a few haggard women. Baggage of all kinds was piled on behind. I looked at it. I looked at the young man and the women. I didn't have to say much. They saw that I could go no further. Compassion is not as rare a thing as many people believe. But until we experience it firsthand, it doesn't make an impression. Calloused as we are, we think ourselves equal to those offering it. This is the fruit of our numb desperation … The women offered their hands to help me up. They allowed me to choose my seat.

I approached the most massive trunk on the wagon. "Go

ahead," they said, "you can have a seat there if you're not afraid, there's a snake sleeping inside."

They even opened the lid for me without hesitating. There it lay amid rags, oblivious to itself. Yellow, green, a little red (devilishly, I thought), snake stripe after snake stripe ran along the creature's body. And it was wound together in twists and turns, the symbol of its pathless paths. Dust, desert dust, homeless dust, and yet it seemed a royal dust compared to what I had been faced with here. For what did it matter if I feared the snake or not, it already lay spellbound by its own nature, which men had transformed into an invisible prison. I shuddered. But not on account of the snake. I stared at it for a long time, until the colors grew dull and my fantasy faded.

The trunk was covered up again. The lid was carefully closed. I took my seat.

The wagon rattled. Behind me the dust was stirred up. It surrounded me. I lay down on the trunk, surrendered to the shaking and to the dust and to the snake.

I was almost asleep, just resting on my arm. Hunched over, another bicyclist raced by us. Everything stood still: the country road, the poplars, our wagon and the hill. Only that one man was moving forward. Already he was disappearing into the infinite distance, still hunched over beneath the sky. Wherever could the devil be headed? ———

Part Two

When I think of the expulsion from paradise, it seems to me that it was really not so long ago. It is a good story, a comforting one. It is more comforting in the telling than in reality. There is much in it that has been passed over in silence. For it is no longer the affair of only two, or of many, or of a whole people, and the tribes descended from them ...

The way that it begins now, every day, with each new human life, it is the affair of a single person. (Not a chosen one. You mustn't misunderstand me.) It can be a woman going about her own small business somewhere, it can be a poodle, a tree. Something must fight its way through to that childlike state of "solitude." A certain humility must be learned, a lowliness that ends in nothing. And paradise? Paradise is uncertain. We had it in the beginning—at least we brought it with us. Each of us must take care not to use it up to exhaustion. He must retain at death the happiness of having lived. He must shut his eyes on this thought. That is the palm tree visible even from this world, that is the Gloria exhaled into the heavens.

The wagon drew to a halt. We disembarked. The people had

to go to the mayor's house. They had to negotiate with him, so that he would allow them to ply their trade here in this place, to earn their money.

And perhaps he wasn't happy about it, since many such travelers passed through. I could continue on my way. I went to a tavern. Where else could I have gone? Here there were only houses, each with its own small fate. The tavern was the only place on the road for someone like me.

The garden was dusty, and also dark. Even on this sunniest of days, it was like night here. And it was empty here, too. I looked for a place to sit. That is to say, I took refuge at one of the tables where no one was sitting. This is my way.

But now there was nothing more to do here. A long, unfillable stretch of time seemed to await me. Then I looked up, further back into the garden. A figure—I've thoroughly forgotten what sort—was carrying a meal to one of the seats in the shadows. Someone was sitting there. I hadn't noticed. Even now I didn't notice right away. That figure was blocking my view. There was only a quiet cough, a sort of apologetic announcement that a guest was present.

In the meantime I had grown thirsty, and was truly in need of a meal. The dust hadn't fully sated my hunger and thirst. And now we could see each other. The guest and I: it was death! Yes, it was death! As much skin and flesh still clung to him as to a dying man. Only his hours were numbered. But perhaps they had been numbered for years and months. Consumptives die slowly. The way that he sat there in the dark, though wrapped in a raincoat, he was death himself, to put it kindly. I was close to crying. I think I let out a few sobs. Then I pushed my food away. This man had cut me to the core, so to speak, or to what my core was back then. Because sometimes the core is a person's head, or even his magnetic, fire-feeling hair; at other times it can be the hands or the chest (for working men) or for women, when nothing oppresses them yet, their all-embracing arms. But that was not my core. And all of this had only been a reminder of death and his appearance. I had just wanted to seek my pleasure as others do, to have a meal as usual. Then death had come. And he didn't go away again, as he does in the legends. He stayed. That is to say, each time this meal came round again, the only meal I would have really wanted, there he was again as well. But that is always the way. Everything here proved itself with deadly certainty. (Back then I also learned the word for that.) When life deprived me of all those carefree joys, it gave me in return the weightiness of every loss. With time, I learned to value this loss more dearly than the richness of life itself, which nature, I thought, had provided so generously for me.

And yet you shouldn't screech at me, like those birds whose words one suddenly understands: screech into my life that this knowledge of suffering was payment in advance of my wages for this lifetime. I had to pay it all back, again and again, with each daily recurrence. The same realization that had lifted me up on the first day pushed me to the floor when it returned again in the days that followed. I hardly even heard or saw it anymore, it was simply there. It, I say: meaning myself—and death—and the many other things existing all around me, even if their existence was a doomed one. Then again, perhaps it was not wholly doomed, for we do not by far live long enough to judge of that.

There was a screeching outside, a senseless noise that probably always began here around midday on a holiday's eve. The circus horse trotted by. It wore a caparison that could move you to tears.

Then all at once a frightful din arose: pigs. It must have been feeding time. Across the way was a low wooden farmstead, built in a square, where their pen must have stood. And in the midst of all that came the plaintive sound of a child's toy, likewise square in shape: a small pig bladder that dies again and again, its four enfeebled feet giving way. It was a real carnival. Only there was something ominous behind it. Only there was a bit too much dust. And actually no people, no spectators, respectable patrons of these pleasures. Just peasant people, eating dust.

I stood up, repulsed by my meal. Suddenly I had forgotten the guest. The whining of this little pig bladder made me so weary, with that large, real ruckus behind it. And the midday hour that breaks your strength ... But what should I do now? Maybe I should sleep? We will try anything when we have nothing left. True, it was a glaringly bright day. And only when I entered my little room did I see *how* bright it was. The day seemed to have come into my room to stay. And while perhaps outside, as dusk approached, each thing that had senselessly called its own name throughout the day would gradually forget, and the moon would rise again over rooftops and hilltops and play with the poplars as if with fountains, up here in my room everything would remain the same, undisturbed. It had to stay that way. The bed here, the table, the candlestick (which served no purpose), the walls themselves, they had all stored up so much sober reality that nothing could overcome them. This reality was the lord of the place. And so I, too, did not stir. I even opened the window.

Weary as I was, I stood at the window and waited. Perhaps for the night after all, perhaps the night of sleep? I didn't know. I stood there looking down. Finally I understood: it was the farmyard with the pigs that interested me so much. And at the same time I thought of many other things, as we always do when we are miserable. I thought at once of the tavern-keeper's derisive look as I had entered, and of the server's casual chitchat that I had listened to from afar, a conversation with death in a quiet voice. Oh, you never forget a conversation or a look like that, even when it seems that you've taken it in with dreaming ears and dreaming eyes. Oh, and there were so many things I would never forget. I was veritably rich in them. Yet I didn't actually complain about this gift of memory.

After all, I knew of a man who always, always had to live under such a derisive gaze, and no one could even say why. Yes, I had found a man like that right on this spot: a swineherd.

While I watched, my eyes growing hungry, the old farmhand crossed the yard many times.

In his eagerness he moved effortlessly, almost gently, the way I can imagine someone moving even in the hereafter. But he was hunched over, "hunched to death," as the old saying goes; and the things that he touched seemed to be on a level with him, even above him, higher than he was himself, as old and hunched over as he was.

I saw it on that afternoon, and it is engraved in me forever: the love with which he tended the animals, almost smiling as he worked. Of course this smile was mixed with sighs and clearings of his throat, in the manner peculiar to old people. A smile that brought to mind the most aged, and even the animals themselves. Not that the smile proceeded from animal feeling; but rather from sympathy, from love. Oh, you could certainly call it ignorance if you wanted to, most miserable ignorance. And I'm sure that he often ate no better than the pigs themselves. That hard bread must have been like a stone in his toothless mouth. The animals would grunt for it when they saw him coming, I saw that on this first occasion, and many times thereafter. Not only the animals, but the whole town knew that he received hard bread to eat. And like the pigs, no one else knew why.

The tavern-keeper, my tavern-keeper and the swineherd's master, was only the son of the man he had actually served. That actual master, whose servant had outlived him—serving him even in death, so to speak—had been a good and righteous man. The son, however, as often occurs with no explanation or warning: incomparably wicked and heartless. He was a man who took pleasure in those things that cause us horror. It was he himself who gave his servant that bread every day. Every day he recklessly ventured right up to the edge of that innocence. He knew that he could not fall through, that it would bear his weight. For even if there was in the servant a wisdom that saw and felt all of this, it was not of a human kind.

He was too old for that, he was ninety-five years old. And earlier, though you may laugh, he might have been too young. If no one tells you that your childhood has ended, you might not know it yourself.

In any case—I read this in his movements—he complained of nothing but the sudden downturn the estate had suffered, which had left only his pig farm unharmed and undiminished in value. Perhaps it was in this most particular way that he lodged his complaint about the tavern-keeper's rude demeanor. For the tavern was always empty. The only people who came there were travelers, and that dead man, and a poor woman who certainly didn't bring his house any honor. And when they were gone (I followed his thoughts, for you could almost read them right through him)—who would come then?

In the end, the pigsty itself would become the shelter of his harsh master. And he, the ninety-five-year-old man, would be driven out. For the downward slope into poverty and desperation is steep once they have persisted for some time in secret.

But that of all things did not discomfit him, you could read as much from my window.

And that of all things was the mystery.

It is written in the great book, in every passage. He himself was a word from that book. He was a word placed in a particular passage. He was written in the prodigal son.

I thought about it for a long time. Even as the noise below grew and swelled, this simple perception created within me a blessed calm.

And so I imagined the story told in three different ways:

In the manner of the hard-hearted tavern-keeper, in the manner of the simple servant, and in the manner of my own life. Each of us was a story of the prodigal son. But as for when these stories would ripen and fall sweetly into paradise, that no one could know. With this thought, I reverently lay down to sleep. True, it was not yet evening. But for me it was night. I heard a blowing and rustling, and felt that a whirlwind was passing in the street. And then someone propped a ladder against my wall, and pounded in a wedge with a heavy hammer. But I was already far off, I had left myself behind. And then someone, who must have had nails between his lips, shouted a word to the man who was fastening the rope to the wall, the rope the tightrope walker would have to cross…

Part Three

Granted, desperation had never been more than a word
to me, that harshest desperation that tears people apart.
And a person in that state is like an animal we watch at pasture, saying: "If it knew what awaited it, it would bellow and
run away ..." But it doesn't leave its spot. It has another day,
and then another, and then another final day ... Once, earlier, I
had a dog at home, it ran away but it came back, too, just three
days later. So even that comes to nothing: running away ...
We are hemmed in by the world, by everything that supports
us and everything that threatens us. But we don't recognize
it right away. Like the beasts of the field, and perhaps other
creatures as well, we need some movement to bring it to our
attention; a clear, unmistakable movement, in case we haven't
already caught its scent.—

So when I left this place it was not with any intention of
escaping; rather, I kept a slow and steady pace as I started up
the rising path between the hills.

It was an especially brilliant day. And even if the grass and
flowers could take on no more beauty in this rainless season,

at least they were spared from a flowery death up there in the heights, where the air seemed to sing. A little swallow twittered, almost right into my mouth. A lamb came along. As it came closer, its outlines growing clearer and sweeter, I could see that it wanted to be petted. Of course, it turned out that the lamb was not as soft as I had supposed. Its wool was piled up so thickly in spots that it had begun to form ridges; it only appeared as if it would be pleasant to touch. And its bare spots were cool.

Aside from this lamb I encountered a child, a real one: a less common sight than one might think. And up above, on the ridge of the hill, stood a very old shepherd. I took all this in with a grateful heart. But then, from this glorious prospect, I continued down into the valley, knowing full well that this vast view would not remain with me, that temptation has made its home in the heights for ages: the false hope of a life that renews itself.

The house I was to live in had been described to me in detail. And so I found it at once: I could have pointed it out with my finger. The roof, which reached up high and stretched down almost to the ground, covered both the living quarters and a barn. And just when you thought that the birds were coming to perch on the roof, they would dive down into the grass, or disappear into a tree. That's how low the house sat in the hollow.

But the rest of the world didn't see things as I have described them. They drew sharp distinctions, razor sharp, as they say. For them this was one man's property, in distinction to another, poorer property next door, or one of equal value far away. These squares and rectangles spoke to each other in their own loud tongue; this whole landscape was divided up along the axes of human power. There were horses, for instance; I could see them even from afar, a pasture of unharnessed horses rearing up. There was something rich about them, an uncorrupted strength that extended to their owner as well. I would gladly have lived in that farmer's house. But he was not the owner of my house; my owner was a very different man. And he was right next door. An inexperienced eye could hardly have told their properties apart. And I was just such a person. And I had just such an eye. Actually I was still just a child, and I would gladly have gathered up a few of the dice I had cast—and had played away long ago—and swept them back into my cup. But a higher power was playing with me than I had imagined: and he took a serious interest in who won. In any case, it had to be decided. And he made it very clear, except for those few friendly moments: except for the swallow, except for the lamb, except for the shepherd.

I felt that someone was waiting for me down below. I quickened my pace a bit. And truly: a woman was waiting there, in front of the house in the hollow. Bells were ringing in the farmyards all around. It was noon. The church bells in the more distant towns confirmed it. God was there somewhere. With robe and crown, as in the old church paintings. Something in me rejoiced. Something in me had triumphed. But the woman really was still waiting there. Perhaps she was waiting for a child. But the way that her eyes took me in, together with this child who even now failed to appear, there was something otherworldly about it. She knew me, stranger that I was, surely she already knew me well, even if she gave no outward sign of it. She was not a tavern-keeper, if you will, or a baker's wife.

No, as long as I was around her, she remained just what she was: a day laborer. And the first words I heard from her, and the last words I heard weeks later, could change nothing about this station in life; indeed, her destitution and mine were not the same. And whatever would bring us together again somewhere above this world, that too could change nothing, nothing at all about this seemingly insignificant order of things.

That was my arrival at the house. It was a memorable one, and as long as I lived, ate, slept, wrote, read, sang there: I did not forget it. The room that would be mine, that she had shown me after just a few questions, was quite rustic, and so it was good. It was inexpensive, too. And after all, who in this house would have wanted to charge me more than it cost. It didn't belong to them, anyway. The house had been put on the block. A speculator corrupted by the city was just drawing out the bidding process. He had hired this day laborer woman to keep her eye on the property, along with me, a petty tenant. In other words, the fate that was a stranger to me, to which I was a stranger, had briefly carved out a small, friendly niche for me in that place.

Who came to live there after me? No one, I am sure of it: the house was auctioned off. All that I heard now was: the greatest silence, all day. True, a sewing machine ran incessantly. It seemed to speak in short and long sentences, a whole apron in a single breath. Sometimes someone approached a chest of drawers, opened it and shut it again. But that, too, was the silence of work. Not noisy, not disturbing. Over time, though, I wished that I knew this woman who so faithfully tended the hours. I sensed that an imagined, ideal being was taking her place. How it seemed to follow in her footsteps. But then I would hear a sharper step again, the sound of a heel, or a song would begin. Both seemed equally terrible to me, the two seemed to be one. But then we don't sing with our feet, do we? We don't go through our lives in a song, an unnatural song? And life was natural, after all. Wasn't it? Didn't it turn falsehood into truth? Hadn't it always had to endure a struggle, a split, to return to itself?

But with that, the small frayed edge might have been folded down. The stalwart sewing machine began again to hem and hem. It was a joy! And outside a bird was singing, so near that no one could have missed it. (Yet those who live hard come to hate nature; first the birds, then the flowers, and last of all themselves …) The little bird had perched on one of the small casement windows. I was barely breathing. And so the bird, too, grew stiller. It wobbled its tail, lifting its head as if there were a song stuck inside. Then finally it briskly preened its feathers, as after a bath. But beneath the bird there was only the windowpane, and its ripples were fading … A trembling, and it was gone again. And there I was again in all my weight. How alone I was now, now that I had returned to myself! Doesn't this make us envy other creatures? Wouldn't it be easier to be a bird? But for me that was out of the question. I was myself, and even if I had wanted to be better, more beautiful, it was from myself that I would begin. My heart was precious to me; and not only precious, it was sacred. I would have defended it unto death by annihilation. This I would always profess.

So it was on that day. So it was on many days. The things that I lived through were always taking new paths. Sometimes I was indifferent, or even bored. But ultimately every day was a day of life, the living transcription of life itself, so to speak. My own despair and melancholy were inscribed there by my hand. I would have to inscribe my own death, too. I knew that. That sheltered me from many things. Yet despite all that, it was not very easy to live in this house. First of all, as I have said, it was on the block. In our minds it was already mortgaged. How shameful it was, how we lived like outcasts. To have one's bags packed at any moment, day in, day out … What's more, the house had no bell. All the other houses rang their bells for midday and evening, when the bells of the nearby churches chimed. This house remained mute. It simply didn't exist anymore. Nor did it have any livestock, not even small animals. And even if it had … They would no longer have belonged to it.

Only the little garden, its beds lined with boxwood trees, continued to preach of property, of thriftiness and the persistence of life. The scent of gillyflowers and mignonettes floated over from the garden! And the earnest spinach strictly followed the rows in which it had been sown. Little birds lingered by the young heads of lettuce. They seemed extraordinarily happy in this garden. And whose garden was it, anyway? Wasn't it just the little bouquet on a peddler's hat? No, that would be doing it a dishonor. It was hard work. Every day a hand watered it, weeded it, raked the brittle beds …

Sometimes I looked into the woman's face as she worked. Her face was small and withered, but not yet aging. It had black, protruding eyes. Her hair, likewise the darkest, tumbled into this face in an incredible style. It was the Tower of Babel, translated into a most modern and fastidious form. Aside from that she was a country woman. A plain nightshirt wrapped itself loosely around her coarsely striped petticoat. Finally, her shoes, too, stood out as she walked off into the distance. They were faded patent leather shoes that reached to her ankles. When they stood beside each other, they appeared to be on a steep downward slope, or trying to reach something, the way they stood on their very tips. They were dancing shoes, I said to myself. I thought in passing about the sewing machine, about the song. So that was how it looked? Oh God, perhaps I had not yet heard its most twisted trills. Perhaps it had been sung for me as if it were nothing but an innocent school song, harmless provincial entertainment. But this elderly figure outside was something else entirely.

And already I felt: I could not spare myself from her. I did not dare return to the hermit's existence that was always so dear to me—until I had figured out this riddle. I could not be content with a person I had dreamt up and assembled myself; even if she lived, really lived, next door to me, just as I saw. I had to stand in her life, as in an undivided room. She had to cast her shadow into my life. And these two lives had to fight with each other and win and lose. Only then was it more than just a real fantasy, only then was it life itself.

This was the closest thing to me. And it struck me hard. A heavy blow, so to speak. But at the same time it was a calling, and as poor and weak as I was, this made me tremble with eager ambition.

By now the day had given way to evening. The day laborer had cleaned up after my meal. A red hem of sky brushed my windowsill. Like a stream of blood forking in two, the light parted and sank into the corners to the right and left. Night fell. So everything was ready. Now the theater of this life could begin.

I greeted her. (For the first time, since until then I had acknowledged her only with a retreating glance.) And like everything that has been stored up for so long, her reply poured forth almost unbidden, it seemed to roll right up to my feet.

I shuddered to see how quickly the conversation blossomed, how it shot up before my eyes, beneath my window.

The woman was standing there now, already, looking with wonder at my life. That I could accept it. I should have bent it to my will. She was right without even knowing it. For she seemed much smarter than she really was. In essence, everything she said was just petty speculation about a house that was already on the block ... Speculation that promised nothing for her, for me, or for anyone else. But speculation nonetheless. (After all, we all like to bargain over the heads of others.) And so I listened patiently to her questions.

Why I was there. That was asking a lot. I was there because I was alone.

Oh God ... When you ask a stone why it's all by itself; why it has rolled away from the liveliest setting to a lonely place ... I didn't answer her. I almost didn't speak at all that evening. But she spoke for me. And only then was it a pleasure to speak ... So she thought for a long while before answering on my behalf. Prophetically. And all at once she predicted for me, by her own measure, how I would feel:

If I persisted in my solitude, I would never find pleasure in life. I should think it over well. After all, life ought to be good, ought to be right with the world. It was the window curtain, it was the geranium plant. It was the clock and the lamp. It was our bed, our table. It was the door by which we came and went. And if it was not there, this world, then we had only scenery, drafty scenery, and beyond the door was nothing, was the abyss. Our estrangement was there, our dreadful, self-inflicted isolation.

That was what awaited me. And in reality it was already

there, conjured up by her words. Perhaps not these exact words, but the words that I heard, and the words that she uttered, the woman with the Babylonian hairstyle and the dance-worn patent leather shoes.

She had planted this fear in me. But I didn't move. Now it was her turn.

In the meantime, the night had settled in. The fence had drawn up close, as if to join the conversation. The gillyflowers had faded to a sensory impression, the mignonettes were a bouquet held up to be smelled. The spinach, at its slow, emphatic pace, seemed to have retreated into the earth; and the lettuce, in its worldly, superficial way, had long since disappeared. Only the boxwood rows with their twinned trees, with the paths and the beds of the garden, had entered into a bond with the stars. To be sure, this relationship was sentimental, singing, pouring itself out. But it was a bond with the stars nonetheless, and that was no small thing. I looked up solemnly; gratefully. The stars were there. And the mere fact that we could see them was such an undreamt-of, godly gift, a compensation for our solitude …

"Take what you will," I thought, "I want to gaze out of myself and up to these stars. And if this life, lonely as it is, should nonetheless force me to be with another, at least I may do so as myself alone …"

I was content. But the woman, who was sitting on my window ledge by now—I didn't see her anymore, but felt her, more than I would have liked—took me by the arm. "You," she said softly, as if she, too, had heard this word from the stars (of course she was all-knowing, in the everyday sense), "you should have to start your life all over again one day, the way I did in my parents' house. That would put an end to your resistance."

"My father"—she went back that far without even asking me—"my father was a hardworking barber. He died from his job, like all diligent workers do. You have to understand: the outskirts of Vienna. It wasn't easy for him to earn his bread there. Lots of children, too. But my mother was from the country, she didn't make a big fuss about us. We just had to work. And we all made something of ourselves (even the ones nobody thought would amount to much). One of us became a tailor, one a glazier, one a head waiter, a barber, a cobbler, and one has his own ice cream parlor. Please, you have to understand: all that without a penny. That's no small feat. And he was proud of us, my father. I was his youngest daughter. I was supposed to learn to sew. He always liked me the best."

As she spoke, she looked down at me in the dark, very proudly. I hadn't had all that. (Oh, how she knew that! My childhood, which had lacked such hard-working models, withdrew again into itself.)

"You see," she preached (shivering, she had already wrapped herself in the boxwood garden like a coat, and borrowed the distant stars for herself—the things these people can do), "you see," she preached, "it's always valuable when you can do something like that." (She must have meant her skills.) "Anything at all can be useful. I wouldn't have thought that singing and playing the zither would be worth anything to me, those songs and dances that I'd only learned to pass the time." (And she didn't spare me a taste of these talents.) By now I was standing in complete darkness. But she was growing ever more visible; how? Her voice took up a song, and her fingers moved as if they were plucking a zither. It was the far-off song of an organ man, like the songs that the blind may still sing on Fridays in the rear courtyards of Vienna. I listened. I forgot that it was her. The starry night was there again, the undreamt-of grandeur up above. Did it have to grow so beautiful, so that the flowers could fade to darkness and the birds fall silent? I sang, quietly, but without melody.

Then my neighbor took me by the arm again. It seemed that she still hoped to convince me before the night was through. I listened closely.

She was still telling me about her house. It must have been a real home to her. Next to the washroom was a small "sitting room," as she called it. That's where the zither stood. They liked to hear her play, especially on Saturday evenings, before Sunday came. Then the little shop bell on the door would ring and ring. And many a guest stayed longer than he'd intended. And so it happened that she didn't continue with her sewing. "Things pull you away," she said. "Especially when you're young. What do you know about careers at that age! You only want whatever makes you happy." And leaning into my room, she continued: "I became a zither player, and then a singer in a variety show. And I learned lots of tricks from the sleight-of-hand artists and the acrobats." I listened intently. I must have hoped to learn something, too.

There was a feeling in the air as if the whole world were one great marigold. Some fireflies were coming to life. What was night to them? One of them flew off after another ... But this creature there next to me changed even that night. From that single marigold she made many hardy little flowers for her old-age hat. And the fireflies would have to light her way home, light her way home as quickly as they could at this late hour.

Where in all of this was the truth of truths, where was the

blessed night? If it offered itself to everyone … To this woman here and everyone … I felt ashamed. It's a strange thing for a poor person to feel ashamed on behalf of the night, or of the sky. But this neighbor creature was still standing there. She felt no such thing. She was already trying out a new song. The spirited voice of her youth was gone. The zither was gone, too. But there was something of the carnival in her voice. Something she didn't want. She never would have admitted it to me. But suddenly I heard it in the midst of everything; I too was sharp-witted once.

"She could never have a child, for all the world," I thought to myself, secretly taken aback. As she stood there before me, visible and invisible, she was the least childlike thing imaginable. She could never have been even the shadow of a child. And yet … Where were order, confidence, and truth in human nature, when it was so deformed? And wasn't I her exaggerated counterpart: the exaggeration of truth?

It was night now. Night. It no longer gave freely of itself to anyone, nor did it willfully withdraw. Only we ourselves played the part of the righteous there; to our own misfortune, perhaps. I was tired, I didn't even know how tired. And yet I could not leave this place. As heavy as I felt, I was spellbound, and I had to follow the course of this strange being. A little owl was already hooting. A bird cowered with a fearful cry, as if the predator had already grabbed it by its throat, but perhaps that was only in a dream.

Dream, song, and sound wove themselves together; they followed each other like the fireflies. It was not a proper state of affairs. This singing and flying and dancing was a job for birds, flowers, and butterflies, for fireflies perhaps, but not for people. Least of all for people like this, life was through with them before it even began ... Oh, this creature of the outskirts. Something in me cried out. Perhaps it was my weariness.

The fog was moving in the fields like a herd of distant sheep. The wind drove it onward. One hour gave way to another.

But my neighbor was not at all tired that night. She talked on and on. She recounted the years to me. That is a task of its own that not everyone can do ... How she collected money in the dish, and passed it out again. How each profit was divided into smaller profits. And how each day's profit became so small that it hardly sufficed for more than half a day. "Often," she said in such a terrible way, "the day was only half dressed." Of course by that time singing and dancing were no longer singing and dancing. And the family back home had honest trades, only she was still traveling around in smaller cities and market towns, almost on the street ...

So you could hardly be surprised at the way that she had slowly cut my great marigold into smaller bits. She told me bluntly: she had decided to marry. It had occurred to her all of a sudden. I felt I could see that evening in the little garden, when she made her decision. As if she had brought the garden here to me. A hunchback sat at the table beneath the chestnut trees. He was the one who fancied her. Oh yes, he fancied her. He had eyes. Not eyes for today and tomorrow, many people have those. He had eyes for the duration of things. "Look," he said to himself, "the dance will soon be over. The song will soon be over. But life lasts longer than a dance or a song. Maybe she can see that. And if she can see that, she will see me, too."

With that, he stood and left. But whenever there was another performance, he appeared again beneath the trees. And once he even wore a flower in his buttonhole.—(A wind began to blow, as if it were already combing our hair for the morning.)

But she had other things on her mind by then. And anyway, she couldn't have seen everything that was going on. But again and again, in one way or another, new events cast doubt on her plans for the future. For even if she and her small troupe did not belong to the respectable society of the smaller cities, the people of those cities still came to see them. To see her most of all. She had a special act. She wore a blue velvet dress and tossed out golden stars. They always liked that the best. They clapped so much then. Once they even brought her flowers. That had never happened to her before. There was one man in particular, she described him in detail. A big man with red hair. He had really grown attached to her. He took care of the troupe. The wine always came from him. And he was always sitting in the front. A real man. A proper man, you could see that. She wove him into her thoughts, thoughts she had entertained for some time. He wasn't one of those unsound types who wants to be paid in advance. He had thoughts of his own. He wanted to marry, too. Her, to be precise. In her mind a proper wedding had already been arranged. The hunchback had been cast out. That is to say, he sat in the shadows. The paper lanterns swung their restless, colorful heads in the storm. And between them the stars, which this aging girl gathered and gathered. It was truly amazing.

The morning of the dance, she was prepared to make it serious, she told me. She was done with this life, this halfway disreputable business. And she didn't want to marry a hunchback. She wanted to marry someone who was healthy and had strong limbs and a profitable, respectable trade. This was the man she wanted to marry. There was no question anymore.

The hunchback was forgotten. Let him play the fiddle at her wedding! He was just a humble music teacher in search of his daily bread, something the other man already had: he was a butcher. That was easy to see, and not just any butcher, but a most able one. His shop was always filled right up to the steps with gossiping girls. And even if no daughter of a respectable house would have taken him (for a butcher is a slaughterer, and a slaughterer's work is at the outer limit of the honest trades), still he could be a proper husband for her, she who had already played with the stars, and could no longer pass for a respectable child.

And she wanted to have a place within that world. She felt that more and more. Within it, not outside it, where she had cast me in her prophecies.

For my part, I stood there freezing. The night had laid it all down, its fog, its shadows. It was a moonlit day. The moon had become the sun of this night. My hand was silver, resting uncertainly on the window post. I felt my eyes themselves becoming moons. Sleep came.

But as if she wanted to kill me, this woman who stood with her back to all that splendor, she kept talking on and on.

She told me of the night she called her bridal eve. She told me of the dancing. There were even fiddles playing. A very fine fiddle was playing, a homemade, sensible fiddle.

Now the tables had turned: they became the audience for once, and the others were only musicians. Even if there was one among them who was better than the rest.

Oh, and now this desperation should come to an end. She couldn't take this humble life anymore, this scraping by. This desperation should come to an end. How they could dance.

That was a real bridal eve, that night.

My neighbor looked deeply, searchingly into my eyes. Had I guessed it? Suddenly she wanted to spare herself the words. I didn't know why. I had fallen asleep standing up, like an animal. I had been absent. Only for a moment, of course. Moments of sleep at night are like the distance from star to star. On unsteady legs (for her words had taken the floor out from under me, down to the last little speck), on unsteady legs I saw her standing before me, the woman with her hairstyle, her little jacket, her shoes, just as I had imprinted her on my mind. I felt that I was swaying back and forth, but she was immovable.

Yet it amazed me that she was still there. Hadn't thousands of years gone by?

The clement night held mignonettes and gillyflowers before my face ... I breathed. Deeply.

Meanwhile the people danced on in some garden. I saw them making their noise and turning in circles, my neighbor hardly needed to say more. For her eye was still on that one word that she didn't want to say. She was positively waiting until the dance and drunkenness had reached an unnatural pitch. Until the word sprang from her lips of its own accord, from those lips that now seemed so sober ...

In the end, it was a woman from her own troupe who said it first, this word. And she could see at once that it was true, she could tell from the way that the dance stood still, that her own partner suddenly went limp. "Hangman," someone from her troupe had said.

And then, as if no one had understood yet, the guest continued:

"Yes, hangman. Before you were a butcher, you were a hangman. That's why no respectable girl will have you. That's why you have to marry someone from our troupe. Yes, you were a hangman, hangman, hangman."

The world seemed to spin. Oh—laughing, I watched a star fall. Silently, perhaps it fell into this garden ...

But it appeared she didn't want to wait, my neighbor, she gave no indication of it.

She kept on speaking, but in a quiet tone, as if otherwise we might really miss the sound of a fiddle, she continued:

"The respectable groom could tell at once that the dance was over. That is to say, I kept dancing for a while by myself, but a different dance: I fell ill. For three days and nights my dreams followed one and the same course. I dreamt I was dancing with my hangman. Then his head fell off. But he kept dancing on and on with me, without his head. But then the dream would begin again. And even in its beginning I could always feel the end. Oh, God only knows what I suffered in those three days and nights." Yes, those were her words. And as horrible as they were, I have rarely heard these words spoken so beautifully.

Then I went to sleep. That is to say, I lay for hours in my bed, with the moonlight streaming over me. I hardly knew anymore whether I had dreamt or whether it was true. Only as the light of day itself slowly restored me like a sick person to health, and woke me (for its meaning is not always the same), did I see that it had not been a dream.

And once this was clear to me, I resolved to be on my way. For this certain knowledge of hers, this way of becoming common, this melting together of many into one, had suddenly become repugnant to me. And within me I heard a voice, as if I had not recently spoken these words myself, as if someone else were comforting me with my own words: "I was myself, and even if I had wanted to be better, more beautiful, it was from myself that I would begin." (And little by little the moonlit night inside me was ebbing.) One ray of sun after another broke through the steel mantle of the morning dew. I left money for the day laborer. Then I left the house, silently and in a hurry, as if it were my last chance …

When I had arrived at the bottom of the hill, where the path meets the road, I encountered a small hunchback. He was pushing a bicycle with one of his elongated hands, and in the other he held a fiddle or a mandolin, wrapped in cloth. From the way that he turned the bicycle, I could see that he meant to go in the direction from which I had just come.

The sun was bathing itself in the shadows. The shadows in the sun. I could hardly tell a real bird from a flicker of the light. Just a fervent chirruping—did it come straight from the heavens, or from the field itself?—pounded in my heart. Now only my memory believed in the course of the past few hours, in the footstep from the room and the rattling of the never-tiring sewing machine. But all that I could see was a brown line, the roof over all of those experiences … And finally, a shepherd loomed up into the sky like a star from the heights above. For what is God's will, but that we should be reconciled to ourselves.

The Old Tavern Sign

Some years ago, in a hidden corner of Styria, there stood an old tavern. There it stood, where no one would ever have hoped to find it. It stood there with its single story, as if it had been left vacant, like an etching made by one soul to tell another just what a house really is. But above the door hung a sign emblazoned with a magnificent stag. With its front legs it was springing into the forest, while its back legs lingered behind, allowing a church spire and several houses to peek through. A whole world, with a hunter kneeling at the other end, so small and insignificant, a shotgun in his hand. He aimed and aimed, as if it had only belatedly occurred to him, when the stag had long since leapt away. (So it goes for men at times, and not just with woodland game.) But of course this image was only meant to depict the power and grandeur of the animal, and to imprint the house more firmly there in its meadow in the middle of the woods, this house that claimed to be a tavern. Yet no one but a hunter and forester, or a coal burner, or perhaps a mountain shepherd heading home, could find his way to this uncharted place; and then it wasn't for wine or beer, but to breathe the vapors of a glass of schnapps poured from the large clear bottle. Then silence would follow, since no one else was there anyhow, except the deaf old woman who always left the glass and the bottle to her guests, because she couldn't pour those drinks drop by drop anymore without shaking and trembling. In fact, she must have been almost blind, too, because the one time a stranger actually came and asked her to pour him a glass, not knowing the customs of this tavern, she poured it right onto the table; carefully, to be sure, but right onto the table. Nor did she speak as she went about her business, there wasn't any point, she was deaf. She was empty like a vacant house, where you call and call and no one comes. She was deaf. And she was so old that a great-grandson of hers, already grown, could remember the quavering lullabies she had sung beside his crib. She was so old that it seemed death had started his count high for her, and would keep on counting, up to a hundred or more. Oh, this woman was a wonder. Did she do anything? Indeed, she did. She did just what needed doing in a nearly lifeless house like that. She laid a fire in the hearth and whipped the porridge into shape. There wasn't much else to eat in her house, except the milk that a little shepherd boy brought every morning and evening. Of course her people sometimes drank schnapps, too, but that wasn't her way. She seemed to serve life just as life served her. But she hadn't dealt with the cattle in quite some time. The men took care of that, the grandsons and the farmhands who were around the house in the morning, at noon, and in the evening. They yodeled now and then, too, but mostly for themselves and the fields and the Alps, those heights to which they aspired; and the old woman didn't set the bowls on the table any faster or straighten the chairs when the men were drawing near, because she didn't hear them. For her there was only one time, and it was within her; an ancient time. It started early and had no need for sleep. God knows how many clear, moonlit nights had already made their home there, at the small window of her room. And besides, there was rarely anything out of the ordinary. What was there, was there. And mostly that was work. You would have thought all of these workers were little old men if you didn't see them in broad daylight. But they were just men of few words, peculiar men. Every now and then one of them would stray off to a dance floor or some other spot. But that was only on jubilee days when the whole country was on the move: around carnival and at harvest time; then no one asked why they had come, these men everyone had forgotten. And when they left because they didn't like it there, no one asked after them then, either. For the women at the dances are common property (unless a man picks one out for himself and won't let her go, and buys her wine and roast; but then before he knows it he can find himself waiting late into the night). Life always holds a special charm at the height of pleasure, a summit that responsibility and obligation and duty and guilt seem unable to attain. Where there's nothing to do but dance and stamp your feet, now with this woman, now with the next.

But when someone abstains from such things, that's not so easy to believe. People think he's just gone off to dance somewhere else. And if it should happen that he's taken a special liking to an old, forgotten Bible and the mysteries it reveals in its letters and images, inside and out: well then this Bible is his chosen one; and he may dance with it all the way to heaven. For as hard as life is, weighed down with men and the burdens they have to bear hither and yon, and with the clods of earth stuck to their clumpy shoes; even if life is hard, still, in some invisible, unknown way, it is rapturous. Truly, somewhere in this life there is still music playing for the dance, even if we have not quite found its pace.

It is a tempo that sweeps us blissfully along, usually in love. In love with a person, or with money, or with work. Of course it can be hate, too, malice. That doesn't matter. It can also be stupidity and thoughtlessness, that too is a sort of rapture. Regardless, it is something that has taken hold of us, something we have taken hold of, visibly and invisibly.

And so it is no surprise that one of the men sitting there in the darkening room suddenly found himself lost in thought. At first, he started puzzling it out.

"That couldn't be," he said to himself. For marriage was a lifelong endeavor. You loved someone you thought was properly suited for your entire life. Someone who would still blow out the lamp when she was old and deaf and everyone else had gone to sleep in the dark. You loved with the seriousness proper to certain questions in life: whether to buy another piece of land, whether the house really needed a new roof, or if it could be patched for another year. The same seriousness applied to deciding what was needed inside the house. But the fear there is greater, since people are subject to change. And before you know it, you're a different person, too. You're not in the same place as before.

This last thought troubled the farmhand the most. It troubled him because his love was so different than he had reckoned.

This love had been there for a long time. But he had never realized it. It was the old horsekeeper who had first brought her into his house. Right into the house where he lived: you could hardly hope for anything better. But it soon became clear that this was a love of a different kind.

For the child that the old man had simply set down in his house was feeble-minded. The basket was leaning against the wall; to him, the little boy, it seemed like a house in its own right. And the two-year-old creature sat on a stool, her little head leaned on a chair that someone had placed there: free of sadness, of pain, of joy and devotion. She was so lovely, sitting there in her soulless splendor, that at first no one asked anything else of her.

But that was just the danger. That allowed her to find room in human hearts, where she would not have found any otherwise. And the boy made sure that nourishment was not lacking there. Because first of all she was wordless like everyone else in the house, and then the little creature was also truly beautiful. And that was something new.

At first that seemed to be enough. After the horsekeeper had fed her some porridge, he set her back in her basket. She crouched there again with no sign of impatience while the old man repacked his pipe; she was neither person nor thing.

Back then the bullfinch was still alive, too, that nimble and joyful bird (it's said that such a bird can die of joy), and the boy would really have liked to know if the little girl hadn't heard it. But already the old man was standing at the door and banging and wheezing, with that beautiful nothing, with his stick resting jauntily on his shoulder. And they were alone again, and life wasn't made for thinking too much about that sort of thing.

That was years ago. It had happened several times since. At first the child had grown very slowly. Four years were like two. But then, when he saw her again much later, observing her now with a curiosity he concealed (though in fact he'd run after her as she went home from the horse pastures with the old man), she seemed to have grown into a wonderful flower of paradise: like a life-sized gentian. (It's a mysterious thing about the human body: the sleep of the soul sometimes does it such good. Once I saw a young man, a twenty-four-year-old, who suffered from the falling sickness; he was endowed with a holy purity worthy of the body of Christ. But when he slept he looked like the god of love. And his four and twenty years appeared no more than eighteen, untouched and innocent as they had been.) It was the child, a young woman now, who brought this wondrous boy to mind. I could imagine her becoming his Psyche. She was barely seventeen, perhaps even younger. Her body was white as snow from always sleeping in the shade. And her head, with a pile of hair pinned together on top, was motionless, almost aloof.

To be sure, it was soon clear that she didn't actually look at anyone, she didn't even look at the animals as they passed by with their billowing manes. And she could not have missed them, if she'd had a soul at all. But the animals knew her and loved her. First one, then another enjoyed the company of this senseless, idle nothingness. When the child drank from the artesian well, animals liked to come too, to quench their thirst alongside her. And often the girl lay between two horses as they joyfully rolled in the flowers. Other times one of them would come from behind and press its head against her back, as if it to push her up the mountain, and yet another time one of them thoughtfully touched its mouth to the girl's head as she sat with her hair undone, staring blankly forward.

And so it was no surprise that someone should not only find her lovely, but actually love her. For even if something warned against it, as if it were a deadly sin to love a soulless creature, even if instinct bore out these whispers of conscience: still the same girl was there as before. She was the child of a wealthy farmer, which only added to the reverence with which she was regarded. For her that meant that she was not pressed into service, not forced to acquire a consciousness she didn't have: that consciousness that so terribly transforms young beasts of burden, and makes them into something quite unlike animals—into something truly low. Quite the contrary. Indeed, in a less apparent sense she was more than just a person. Her undisturbed, beautiful way of life lent to her movements a degree of perfection that we may never have seen before in this natural form. In the city, her affliction might have been accounted a mental illness. But here in the country she was feeble-minded, simply feeble-minded. And whatever she did, in its momentary infinity it became a landscape, always newly created. The farmhand, in any case, was thinking of her. And that was all he needed to do, for days on end. That was enough for him.

That autumn he would not have gone to any of the church festivals, even with the most beautiful living girl around, simply out of sorrow for this one dead girl. For even if she was still living, breathing, he told himself that she was dead, was damned. And yet she was not damned in the truest sense. It was simply that her soul had remained in a vegetative state. Though she drank from the well, she did not feed herself. As the flowers are fed by heaven, so she too required feeding, by a human hand. Otherwise she would have grazed from her plate, just as she drank from the trough. But as it was, she sat at the feet of the old horsekeeper. And the old man, with a sort of reverence, would dip the spoon into the copper pan as it sat on the stove—country habits still held sway around the horse pasture—and place it in the child's mouth. Sometimes he stroked the girl's hair, or held her two limp hands in his hairy, scarred, old-man's hand.

At such times he was especially aware of how much she needed his protection. More than the horses, which often fought to the death in the moonlit field. It kept him up at night, so to speak. And so, too, he had to make do with two of the farmer's younger children in place of the farmhands he might otherwise have had, and he accomplished his great task alone, with their meager assistance.

He had already felled many trees with his own hands, and dragged them to the drinking trough to channel water, and at times he nearly disappeared beneath a load of hay as he carried it uphill, wheezing, as if he himself were a mountain of grass. Although he was small by nature, he acquired a certain stature from the duties he had taken on. The little man would have hanged himself at once if the girl had suffered any harm. I don't mean to say that her death was out of the question. All men must die, the horsekeeper told himself, and this creature could only rest comfortably in God's hands. But an inner fear seized him at times when he thought that he might die before the child. And so he climbed higher and higher into his old age, and perhaps he was already as old as the woman in the tavern below, in the lonely valley, perhaps she too only postponed death because she knew no one who could do her job.

He sewed clothes for this child. He fastened her boots in cold weather. And when it rained for days, he even gave her his own hood, and then looked about with amusement.

But he held no illusion that she was devoted to him. She did not know the danger of fire and water. She feared no abyss, as he had learned to his horror; she knew neither her parents nor anyone else. She seemed to stay with him only because he protected her, because the dogs protected her, indeed, because even the horses guided her homeward. And all this, when it became known, only fed the general curiosity about her. Girls spoke about her to each other, in jest or in horror. But the farmhands for the most part stayed silent, for such things cannot be spoken of.

So this young man, too, in the small, lonely tavern, said nothing of it. Oh, it choked him. The mere thought of it choked him, as if he had already done the deed. After all, it was an evil deed. Even if it was done in love. For who in the world would believe this love. And the world is the mortar that holds together the building of humanity. And since this is all that there is, it seems, anyone who did not think as the world thought must necessarily feel cast out from it. Then, too, he was a senseless animal, but not a beautiful, finely formed one like the girl.

And this young man above all, with his careful respect for traditional ways, would have preferred to remain single rather than to marry a contemptible or otherwise pitiable thing. Without knowing it, he was possessed of a small, strong, nameless ambition. But it was thoroughly disguised as custom and habit. So he wore his sturdy lederhosen and a stiff, gray jacket with an open shirt. And this made him somewhat reckless, somewhat spoiled, though he did not know by what. At the same time, he was somewhat timid, too, always cautious in his deeds. His fellow farmhands mocked him. And yet they feared him, too. He hadn't liked this year's carnival, or else it hadn't liked him. Otherwise he would have gone back ... (So they spoke, at times, among themselves.) But to him they said nothing. And they had no need to speak to him, either, it was easy enough to see what they all thought in these matters, and that was enough for them.

Besides, when a young man seemed so alone, one could never know …

Unfortunately, right now he had just been pulled in by love like a top. It set him spinning, and he danced. And he shouldn't come to rest: that was the object of this game.

At night the whinnying of a horse would wake him, though he had no horses of his own. And in the morning, when all the men set off to threshing, he felt drawn to the horse pasture. But what this meant was: so and so many hands were needed for threshing, and everything had to run like clockwork, as if these hands were the grooves of a single mill wheel. And no one had ever sought to be excused. It would be crazy to do so without some reason, perhaps an illness. And love was no excuse for missing work. Love was for the evening hours. And even then, only real love. But this love was no love at all, so they said, and so he could hardly hope to go …

The young man was terribly tormented, and yet he was far too pure-minded to entrust this unwanted secret to anyone else. (Besides, he hoped to suppress these thoughts.) When he entered his house, he felt he was going to his grave. When he went to the threshing floor, he felt no different. Even when he set to mowing, he felt no joy. Strangely enough, at home it was his grandmother who tormented him the most. Perhaps she reminded him of the girl in the horse pasture. From her, too, he had hardly ever heard a word. She, too, simply lived on without knowing it. She, too, was unlike other women. And so, as he grew day by day more conscious of his love, he began to avoid his own house whenever he could. When the last Ave Maria had been said, he pushed his wooden farmer's chair aside like a bowling pin and went outdoors, where he felt no better.

Then his defiance returned. "I *will* go to the horse pasture." But when he had said that, he felt only dread, and he did not say it again. Instead, he said the opposite, that is, he slightly changed his words. "Why *should* I go to the horse pasture, anyway?" (As if unaware of his own love.) But if he didn't know this love, it surely knew him. It always recognized him. It was practically watching him. It knew if he lifted the pitchfork, how he lifted it, whether he took large steps or stood still, where he stood and dreamt. And when he slept, it took the power of his dreams for its own, and dreamt for him. He was climbing a fir tree, up to the top and then beyond. He didn't even notice that he was past its tip. And so he fell over it, down to the ground, and lay there with dream-shattered limbs, on the edge of the forest, under the tree, and yet in his bed, and it was night, or morning. It didn't matter, anyway. When he awoke it all felt to him like the pain of his unfathomable passion. And his small room, which he had never really seen before (it was just a modest room for sleeping; it was like a coffin, too, as narrow and low as could be, to keep out the deep winter that never seemed to end), he regarded this room now with almost hostile eyes. He saw how a figure entered the room, that figure whose very existence he wished to deny. He laid her beside him then in his thoughts, and felt a visceral horror, as in the presence of a lifeless lover.

But then, as if this had exhausted all his powers of thought, he suddenly turned his roving eyes to a fly that was buzzing excessively loudly through his room—as if his heart had not already suffered the very worst. And often he would cleanse himself then with holy water. But then, in one of the nights that followed, he would dream of a scarecrow, stretched out. Then it would be the girl again. Then it would appear again as nothing but a holy roadside cross.

He resolved to leave this place. Only he didn't know where to go; only he didn't know why. He had never wanted to leave. How would he justify his departure to the others. And there was so much work to be done. They would have to hire a farmhand in his place. He would be hurting them along with his own fortunes. No, to leave … In the end it would only reveal to them that he was in love. And with whom … Better to stay, then. For whoever would hire him elsewhere might ask, too. And love in its earliest stages is deaf-mute and dull-witted, just like the girl was in reality. Such a love doesn't want to hear or see. Being asked about love for the first time is like being thrown into a river.—

So he resolved to take other action. He resolved it against his own will. He resolved to marry. And why not? After all, he wasn't bound to her. He wasn't bound to this love … It was all his imagination.

And as if the other girls had just been waiting for this moment, he thought at once of this one and that. A mother could hardly have advised him more eagerly …

He thought of a pious weaver's daughter in a village beyond the mountain, past the slopes where the horses grazed. His thoughts rested on her. He couldn't say why. He had only seen her once, perched on her spinning stool, so pale and modest, with a purring, well-fed cat on either side. He had relished that sight. That was the kind of woman he liked, someone who thought of nothing but her work. He didn't like women who were always laughing, who were always thinking something different. Ever since love had taken hold of him, he sensed, he had become quite a strange fellow. It was high time that he remembered this weaver's daughter. And like anyone who has been suffering and finally hits on a sufferable solution, he was greatly cheered by this thought. He stopped his moaning. He was on the verge of telling the others about his marriage plans. But even without being told, those who lived with him had noticed the change. They noticed it in each and every thing he did. And finally, making no effort to conceal his aims, he took out his green jacket, long pants, and jackboots. He could tuck the pants into the boots, since he wasn't fond of those long blousy pants; they looked to him almost like a woman's skirt. He even took out a pocket watch and chain.

He washed himself at the well, as if for Judgment Day. Then he went on his way, without a walking stick, as if he were going to church. And he stuck to the proper route, as befitted such an important matter. He followed the road that led straight through the woods. Now and then he encountered strangers from nearby towns. Or a farmer's wife pulled her skirts closer and greeted him. Or a bird hopped off in front of him with a cry. Or he simply stopped and stood still, because such treks were new to him. His spirits were high. It is always so when someone sets his mind on what seems right to him. Besides, the road appeared as if sown with gold. And even more gold clung to the trees. And among them, perhaps outnumbering the golden ones, and not shining so brightly, stood the fir trees and the reddish trunks of the pines. He felt the air perched lightly on his hand like a ladybird. And one squirrel after another looked with its juniper-berry eyes at this young man as he continued down the middle of the wide road. It was good that the journey wasn't too long for a hardy hiker, otherwise he would indeed have gone astray. For the horse pasture was large, and you could always find your way back there, even without a path. To tell the truth, he still hadn't put the thought of going there out of his mind entirely, but he didn't say so loudly to himself, instead he nobly fixed his thoughts on the weaver's family, who were somehow related to him. And besides, he wanted to buy new scythes in their village, where he'd heard they were less expensive.

Then a doe stopped in his path, far away, but facing him, right in the middle of the road. He had to stop, too. It lasted several minutes. The slender body in its holy nakedness moved even him, coarse as he was, even coarser now. Perhaps he had tears in his eyes (his thoughts had unconsciously followed another path). Then a shower of leaves fell from the trees. Another bird hopped off in front of him. And the farmhand, without knowing how, had reached the end of the forest. He felt the autumn much more strongly there, being accustomed to the fields; he was more at home there than in the most beautiful forest. He saw the church spire. He saw every single house, the weaver's house among them. Now he could prepare for his visit. Again he passed by country people in their Sunday clothes. Again he heard the chiming of the bells. Judging by their sound, the church service would soon be over.

He entered during the benediction. The holy water ran over his forehead like a salty tear. Then the organ began to flow like flowers, roses and dahlias, richly swelling garden flowers. Then a censer, its silver jingling, filled his ears. Then the church emptied. First came the men. They were always in a hurry to leave the church. Then came the little girls, and finally the women. The farmhand looked on. The weaver's wife was there among the churchgoers. She recognized him at once. She invited him to pay them a visit. And so he went first to the grocer, and purchased a quarter sugarloaf and a pound of coffee. Then he went to the tavern for lunch, and after that to the weaver's house. He felt uneasy among all the people. He felt he'd never seen so many people in his life. He was glad that the massive loom was quiet that day in the weaver's shop, that the spools had been laid aside, and only the cats lay purring on the spinning stool, one on each side, as if the girl were between them. They were magnificent animals, well versed in beauty and idleness. They received the sort of generous attention that others lavish on their geraniums. Apart from them, the room was empty. That is, the weaver was sleeping beside the oven. He was wearing short sleeves. His shaven face had a Sunday shine. The young man sat down to pass the time. The clean, bright room made an impression on him. Of course it wasn't like that at home. How could his old grandmother have managed to provide for more than their daily needs.—It was time to have a woman in that household. He was feeling warm and eager. Then the young woman entered, shyly, because she already knew who was in the room, and placed a basket of knit stockings on the table. After a few words had been exchanged, she set to darning. Then finally her mother came to wake her husband. Then everything came alive. The weaver told stories. He told how much linen and half-linen he had woven. He said you could calculate how far it would reach out into the world. Of all the kilometers in the world, he had woven many a meter. For he was seventy years old, and since the age of thirteen he'd been sitting at this loom. If you added it up, you could go quite a distance without even getting your feet wet, quite a long journey under his own roof. He didn't even need an umbrella. Everyone laughed. They almost forgot about the tavern. But they did go in the end, after they'd each had a little glass of schnapps and a warm cup of coffee. Just the men, of course. The weaver's daughter closed the door behind them, half smiling, half blushing. She had understood the purpose of his visit and the pound of coffee and the sugarloaf. No woman was dumb enough to miss that. Besides, she wanted to understand it, since she rather liked the young man. He was quiet like her, and a decent young man, too. She thought this to herself as she took up her knitting wool again, setting aside a mountain of mending behind which she nearly disappeared, silently working. This was a Sunday after God's own heart.

She didn't know where the men had been all this time. It was night when the weaver returned home, and night again— the same night, and yet another—when they went to bed.

Outside all the colors were gone. Only the autumn wind was beginning to rustle now. It was shaking the jewels from its own crowned head. Leaves were raining down. But the country road could still be seen from afar in the moonlight. The moon lavishly cast its woven cloth on the ground at the young man's feet. He could not lose his way. Slightly drunk as he was, this moonlit night was just right for him. It entered his eyes, it led him onward as in a trance. And for a long time that was good enough. But because there was no one on the road, because he met no one else, he began to feel uneasy with

himself. He felt that horror of oneself that comes in the night.
He stopped. (Not to avoid going further, just to think.) Hadn't
he wanted something? Hadn't he planned something for the
way home? He understood at once. He leapt over the ditch almost as swiftly as a stag. Now he could no longer be seen. Now
he could no longer be heard, either. His steps were cushioned
by the leaves that blanketed the narrow paths. Only his high
jackboots with their stiff leather produced a groaning, almost
natural sound, a rattling reminiscent of the sound of deer in
rutting season. It would have been better not to wear those
boots. But he didn't think of that. His only thought was that
he wanted to see that beautiful, feeble-minded girl. Maybe he
imagined that he could carry her off. After all, she was only
an animal. But then he stopped thinking altogether, because
nothing seemed true except that one thing, that he wanted
to have her. He forged ahead with large, reckless steps. And
while he was still an hour or more away, he already felt close
to her. He cherished every leaf that fell on him. A stag belled.
He understood it well. He thought about the doe he had seen
on the way. Now everything was clear to him. Except that the
incidental things now seemed essential, the essential things
incidental. He saw the pastor. He felt the drops of holy water.
The organ's flowery petals scattered down to him. In his mind,
he left that sacred place with a sense of peace, as if he had
prayed for poor souls. Meanwhile, he heard his shoes rattling
loudly, and a deer belling. It must have been a stag, he heard it
now as if nearby. Love had robbed him of his senses. Bodiless,
it held him in its arms—. And as if something were standing
in his path, he moved on only with great effort. He was breathing loudly from his exertion. Now his boots were quiet too, of

course, for he was standing still, listening. But without seeing anything. He thought he was already very close to the horse pasture. Now he heard a dog howling. It must have been howling at the moon. Well, animals have to suffer, too. He looked up into the air. He could hardly see any sky through the gap in the trees above the narrow path. But one star shone through. There was no breeze now. Yet he smelled something. Something strange, something meant for him. "Ah," he thought suddenly, "if only I'd bought the scythes." But then he continued on, a jumble of wine and beer and schnapps and thoughts of all kinds, petty and base. His shoes rattled again. The stags belled. It was coming from many sides.

Finally, there was moonlight. A field lay before him, traversed by veils of fog. And through the middle of the field ran a murmuring stream, in an inconceivable, almost enchanted zigzag. It ran so freely, in such a mysterious course, that its silver gleamed like a gown, sure of its own worth, speaking and sighing, laughing and weeping.

That was the edge of the horse pasture. He stopped, perplexed that it had taken him so long to get there. Wasn't she coming? Anything was possible for such a poor soul. He stood still again. For it seemed to him that something had just been waiting for him to emerge from the forest. He saw: a stag had stepped with him out of the forest's darkness. At first there was only one. Later there may have been four. But this one was following him. He didn't know why. It would have been much too late anyhow. So he kept to a straight path, his thoughts contradicting themselves as they do in times of danger, "they can't be following *me*." Suddenly he was thinking of nothing at all, not even of the girl. But somehow, in a plea for help, he turned in her direction. But from just that point a stag was coming toward him. So he made for the stream. He crossed the stream. By now he had reached the middle of the clearing. But that was all.

The stag leapt over him, as if engaging the man in a wicked joust. "This is the end of me," the young man thought. It had knocked him down. But people being as they are, just after this he was happy again, and stood up. He should have stayed down. Perhaps then the enraged animal would have left him alone. It must have known that he was a man, and not a beast. Didn't it know who he was, that this was him? He was the hunter. He might have a gun, or a scythe. Why wasn't it afraid of those things? (In fact, he didn't have so much as a stick.) But on this night, the animal might have feared nothing at all. It wanted a fight.

It started to fly over him again. But closer and closer, lower and lower. The young man pulled his hat down over his head as he lay in the grass, so that he wouldn't have to watch anymore. For those long leaps were dreadful. The stags (indeed, there was no longer only one) raced over him as if he weren't even there. Or worse, as if he were nothing. He felt their hooves, light but hard on his jacket. He could almost count them. They seemed to be releasing all their rutting fury upon him. Often it seemed that they were gone, but they were only leaping through the lines of fog that floated over the stream, as at first they had only leapt over him. They merely disappeared and appeared again. But then he was only the second hurdle in their race, so to speak, and the third was the heart of the green forest. But they returned, even from there. He was the one—the man lying as if dead on the grass—who gave their leaps a new ferocity.

How many times they struck his head, how many times they brushed his arms and feet, can only be a matter of conjecture.

Once the stags had felt him in their hearts, they did not forget him again. That is where the animal guards its primeval essence. It persists. It charged at him with its bellowing cries. It waged a fearful fight with a defenseless man. Its antlers bore him. Over the stream, over the fog. The stag seemed not to notice the weight. And the shock seemed to have rendered the man not only speechless, but insensate as well. And the animal's joyous wrath bore off his motionless form with its growing strength. One stag would poach him from another. One stag would leap away from another, the quarry held in its broad antlers.

The moon and the stars did not stir. God did not stir. The forest and the fields lay still, as if they weren't there. Only the stags kept surging, with this quarry in their antlers, this man who had vainly deceived them with his jackboots, as if he were a doe, pure and innocent. Their bellowing had ceased. Now the stags were pure joy, empty triumph.

But many a night passes that way over one who is dying and dead.

The sky broke open again with a quiet red line. Dogs brought the first trace of the dead man. They tugged and wagged the old shepherd and his boys to the spot. The horses sniffed at the battlefield. A butterfly landed on the corpse's chest.

As they were tying together a stretcher to bear him, the girl passed by. Without a shudder, without fear, without the slightest sense that she ought to help. She, who had never filled or carried even the smallest jug, walked unsuspectingly beside the old man. Fir twigs and foliage covered the victim. Those who saw him doffed their hats before him, before the majesty of death. No one had to show the old horsekeeper the way.

He knew where he was headed with his burden. Down below, halfway home, where he had always set down the basket with his little foster child, where the hunter was painted on the tavern sign, the stag leaping away from his shot.

The Mouse

Death was prepared in the form of a trap. But before its time finally came, the mouse would have to gnaw through the wall that led into my bedchamber. It would have to gnaw through a long and narrow passage, and gnaw through my sleep.

Sometimes I pounded on the bed with my fist, frightening myself with the way that its thunder rolled over everything imaginable in the night. And I thought I could sense that the mouse felt this fear, too. But before this wave of fright could roll gently into peace, that same quiet gnawing could be heard again from afar. It was so quiet that it was audible only to someone alone and left to himself in a house by a moonlit field on the edge of a forest. He guards himself like his own hunting dog, and even when he is asleep he will hear any approaching danger. He is like fog, when it is dark, the fog that seems to live in its own light. He is like the rain, far and wide, high and distant, in the heavens and on earth. How could he fail to notice the gnawing of a mouse, when that activity returns again to itself. He feels it in his blood. So once again I lit my candle, the bane of all four-footed intruders. But the candle didn't spread its angel wings as it had in other nights, arching them over the dark abyss of fear, becoming a spirit of the shadows, the better to offer its light … Instead it suddenly betrayed me to my enemy, becoming a sort of gnawing creature itself, there in its candlestick. It ate away at my sleep, and the mouse did not fear it.

But so far the mouse was not there with me in that nocturnal brightness. That hour was yet to come. Meanwhile I drifted off and dreamt in the glow of the candle. I dreamt of a city, of its subterranean passageways. Then I awoke again. This stolen night was taking back all the rest that it had given me. The mouse was gnawing, louder than before. The light was still burning. I thundered again with my fist, but only hurt my hand. After that it was quiet, but only as long as the terror lasted, our common terror. And before it had even dwindled down to nothing, before the softest gnawing began anew, I turned in search of help—following once more in the footsteps of infinity, I turned to a sound that obeyed its own law—the clock. It ticked as if its minutes were a game for the stars. I felt at one with it. I listened to it as to the pulsing of my own blood. But then, softer and more distant than any clock, in quiet competition, it began again: the mouse. I almost had to laugh. But no one laughs at night. It's dangerous to laugh at night. Such laughter borders on insanity. O God of insomniacs: You who hinder no plant in its growth (but that You would kill it), You who hinder no raindrop in its fall from the cloud—why do You hinder sleep?

The mouse, if it must, may gnaw, may keep gnawing, night after night, even if the house should fall in upon it. But I, poor soul, must find rest. I covet rest—the everlasting nourishment of the soul—above all else in life. Whosoever is denied rest, to him the night is like day. He hears the winds and waters roaring endlessly in the treetops. For him all roads, even those bright, moonlit roads, lead into the heavens' abysses. He is like a man condemned.

And during the day the sun has power over him, like a moon. He closes his eyes before the sun and feels his way like a blind man through its enchanted world. And thinks only of the evil that the sun has already wrought upon it.

And then, as if these sleepless nights had been prepared decades in advance, he remembers the stories that men once told him of those animals, the mice. Of fields undulating with living waves of field mice. Always leaping from one earthen hole to another, to gnaw at the roots of the crops. That field and all the fields for miles around were laid waste. They no longer belonged to the farmers, or to the plants: they belonged to the mice. And the stories told of this devastation were so terrible that they cannot be told again. And the women all stayed home, they were not allowed into the fields, nor did they want to go. And I thought: when I shall die, how horrible … will the mice gnaw me to pieces, too? And I saw a skull with mice springing out.

Then, as if this human head were nothing but a hollow gourd with a light inside that slowly burns out, an hour arrived at last when I was of no use to the moonlit night, or to the mice: when I could finally sleep. I slept without dreaming. A fleeting sleep, like weather-bleached, straw-yellow grass, a vacuous sleep. I awoke in near-amazement. I remembered only a quavering sound, a trembling that seemed to emanate in miniature from a single point near my bed: but I experienced it in its true enormity, a creature was seeking to escape from its prison! Sometimes it hung with all four legs on the wires of the closed-up trap, as if it felt freer in the air, sometimes its rodent teeth rested impotently on the iron bars. It was indigestible, this prison. It seemed light and airy like no other, but it was nonetheless the prison of all prisons. Even a mouse could feel that, and a man, who can become that mouse's partner in suffering without even knowing how or when (and not for the sake of a morsel of fatty bacon), such a man knows full well what that creature suffers. And so I, too, was at once a part of all this. I grasped it with my eyes, which only seconds before had been asleep. And I trembled inside as well. But reflecting on my agonizing, sleepless night, I smiled with pleasure at the creature's pain. Now its time had come. It had banged away at my night until finally its day had come, at my hand. To be sure, I didn't intend to kill it, although my own rest could only be assured by its death. But I wanted to make the most of its terror, so that perhaps in the future it would give this house a wide berth. After all, there were so many acorns, roots, and berries in the forest. It could enjoy them with the added relish of freedom. Many a root, warmer than a house, could shelter it in the winter. In my thoughts I praised the little animal, I liked it now that it no longer hoped to share my house. I even hurried, for the mouse's sake. I put on my clothes, if only to wash away the husk that this night, the night I had just endured, had sought to affix to me, always and forever, like a hollow mask. And now and then I glanced with concern at the little creature. It had grown still. Its gray, soft fur was bristling. It seemed to be holding something, as all sleeping animals do: itself. That reassured me. I turned to my household tasks. "You need fear no more than you deserve,"

I thought. "I only want to fix my breakfast before I go into the woods." (Imagine, I could think about food even when a living thing had fallen asleep in my house in mortal fear. My first act upon waking was not to set it free. I wanted to have my meal first.) There was no excuse for that: not the fact that it was only a mouse, a mouse that destructively eats away at our stored-up provisions, that bites our clothing to bits when we put it away for the season; not even the fact that it was just a little thing, in contrast to the great big life that I had not yet begun to live out. Nothing made my pangs of conscience seem excessive, exaggerated. It was not just a mouse, it was not just the mouse, it was a creature, a living thing. On the other hand: it was not just some love preached from afar, some game or confusion of large and small: it was my life.

I remembered a cat that had caught the scent of a mouse I had once freed. It was morning then, too. I had stood as if rooted in place, looking down at them. Pearl gray just like this mouse, it had stood on its hind legs and pleaded, in such fear that its eyes no longer seemed to see, they seemed instead like pearls set into an unreal being. It pleaded for its life. It squealed. It gesticulated with its paws. But it did not leave that spot. Its eyes were like little torturous pins, open and darkly glistening. The cat saw that and heard it too, looking past the mouse in apparent boredom, one paw raised in the air. The little creature could not escape, so the cat simply forgot it. Forgot it just as I did now. Much later I saw that mouse again, the mouse that had ventured into my trap on that visit. It had turned to dust. The starved skeleton was a terrible sight, the hind legs stretched far back, the front paws stabbing up into the air. And other things came to mind, too, for we are bound to all the suffering that occurs on our account. It is engraved into our lives. It clings to us like guilt. As if in passing, it magnifies our dealings with this vast nature a thousandfold. If we were guiltless, to be sure, it would be a beautiful, holy sight. Like a shower of stars, it would affirm our life.

At that I returned to the cage, slowly, hanging my head. I already knew: the mouse was finished.

The Old Man

The value of our existence is by no means always a function of its weight. On the contrary, because our fate alone is frequently too light, there are stones, as it were, that we take on as counterweights. And the way that people use them … Some heap these stones upon what is dearest to them on this earth. And others have claimed that they had to swallow them. Ah yes, I know people who look as if they had swallowed stones.

The ashes had been cleared from the oven. And there was even fresh brushwood and a bundle of paper inside. You could see it glowing through the little hole in the freshly polished brass door. But it was not content to calmly burn. It was too cold. The oven had been unheated for too long; the windows and doors had stood open for too long. And now you couldn't even light a match. All the matches in the whole box, rubbed down to nothing, lay on the freshly scrubbed white floor. The old man sat in front of them. Kneeling had drained away all of his strength. And finally, as he tried to light one last match that he had happily found, the cold smothered it again between its invisible hands.

The old man looked around, he listened. Had the young lady already gone home? A light step, moving from the dish rack to the door, told him that she was still there. So he gathered himself together. One truly feels as if in a bone house when such a stiff old man rises again. "Hey you!" he called out, when he had collected himself. He had forgotten her name, even though this creature had been coming at the same time every day for half a year.

She heard him, too. With a hidden, not to say gloating smile (for young people often laugh out of harmless spite at the futile efforts of their superiors), she stood in the doorway, her hard-working hand resting firmly on the door handle. But while she sheltered herself, she directly exposed the old man to a wicked draft. And although he stood still, it seemed as if he were being blown by the wind. He seemed almost inanimate, the way he stood there pointing at the faded fire. One might feel the same way watching an unmanned sailboat cut an arbitrary path through the water.

The windows, which hadn't been firmly latched, blew open again in the draft. The upper windows, they now saw, had been open all along.

But the old man wasn't pleased to see how quickly everything was taken care of now that someone else was in charge: the young maid brought a small shovelful of glowing embers from the kitchen stove, and with that the job was done; it simply burned. And a couple of boxwood logs laid crosswise over the embers gave the whole thing a proper appearance. Surely that would generate heat. But we don't know what a room is like when it has been truly chilled through, much less when it has also served as chamber for dying. Such a room will remain cold, it takes this as its solemn duty.

And even when you think it should grow warm, as log after log is consumed, a cold sweat condenses on the furniture. The mirror grows blind, the pictures obscure. And even the windows can let in no more light, they are clouded as if with breath. The same cold spirit does this that put out the matches' small flame. Or is it just the warmth trying to emerge? So much the worse.

The worst thing of all, though, would have been to slump down on the settee in despair. Its rusty springs would only snap, as if to roughly and rudely cast him off. It was all enough to make you run away.

But the old man stayed where he was, silent and idle, set in his idleness. In fact, his whole existence came down to a sort of nonexistence: to this idleness. And yet he was banal, and real, and it seemed it would not have required any extraordinary effort for him to attend to his daily needs. And he did attend to them, but in such a lifeless way that it could inspire a sort of horror. And it wasn't clear: was the sobriety of his actions the source of this horror, or did this horror of his bear a veneer of sobriety? It must be terrible to be such an old man. It was hard to believe that he was still human.

Now he pulled one of his armchairs, which had been joy-lessly arranged around the table, to the door of the oven and waited for its warmth. Darkness fell. Not until it was pitch black outside did he think to look for a lamp. Out of thrifti-ness, of course. To have both at once was wasteful. The fire had served as a lamp until now. That had practically been its only function. But because this lamp was burning in the oven, it only cast a narrow band of light that ran from the oven's mouth to the closed door of the room, where it pulled up and continued to the ceiling. There its rays flickered down along the chain of a hanging lamp; faintly, just enough to reveal the lamp hanging there empty.

And the old man didn't want to leave the doors to the adjacent rooms ajar when he went out to search for a candle, as you can well imagine. His hands felt their way through the dark rooms, through one after another. There was a lantern in the kitchen, but he didn't find it. Other people had created an order there that only they understood, an order that went its own way, that shut him out. Then it suddenly occurred to the old man that there was a candlestick in his bedroom. It was easy to find in the dark. But he didn't light the wick until he was back in the sitting room—the flame would only have died again and again beneath his hands if he had lit it out there, and he thought it had finally grown warm in the room. The evening stretched on. And the old man stayed on his spot again, almost as before. You couldn't say he was waiting for anything. Except perhaps a certain hour when he would go to sleep. You couldn't say that he was killing time, as can rightly be said of many other people. Perhaps his sin was that he never brought it to life. At least not in the evening, when he was so completely alone. And the world outside was just like his silent room when he finally rose and went to bed. He hardly ever slept. Only toward morning did a bit of twilight enter his gray eyes.

Spring can recede at times, especially in those hours when the earth has grown cold in the night, and the rising ball of fire is not yet radiating strength. Then it is truly freezing. Every young blade of grass is edged in white. Nature thinks back on recent days, and its hair turns white.

As if wearing a cold mask, one lies there and thinks, without any hope of sleep or dream. A dream, above all, is the living mountain of the soul in this otherwise deathlike state. The old man at least had to know that he could neither sleep nor dream. But since he was already in those years when memory occasionally fades altogether, it seemed, at least at times, that he was there and yet already departed. And when he was there again, he was so soberly focused on his daily existence that a bit of pain could even provide a noble contrast.

Every morning he went to an unremarkable little café. At least it was warm there. And there were daily papers lying about. A chance to occupy himself with others' suffering. Oh, this flight from one misfortune into another! Who hasn't experienced it at least once, when falling in the street, if nothing else. That icy joy of others' sympathy. For there is hardly anything else to be found in those faces. These daily papers are the snowball that weak men roll into the avalanches that they take for the life of their soul.

The old man started with the government reports, as usual. And then he proceeded to those pages that depict life in the streets, or give the layout of a house in which something has happened. Then he read about business and the stock exchange. He had nothing to do with that anymore. Or perhaps we can say that he had never had anything to do with it. That was just it: everything was settled. There was an order in his life that could not be disturbed again, thanks to the natural coldness of his character. Only once in his life had he entered into a business transaction (everything else that he owned had been in his family for ages)—that business transaction was his marriage.

The woman in the café poured his coffee, pushing his newspaper aside with the coffeepot. There wasn't much room for compliments there, it was an especially cheap establishment, and the patrons were unassuming. And the proprietress knew that, as people know all such worldly wisdom—and the stronger they are, the more they can turn it to their advantage. And we know, sadly, what sort of people the strong usually are. So the old man drank, he slurped, the brew was still hot. There were rolls in the basket, free for the taking; they also lent the room the air of a bakery, lit up early in the morning. Nonetheless, there were many things, things that were hard to pin down, that kept anyone from feeling at home here. After the breakfast hours were over, this woman wanted nothing more to do with the business. She sat down in the background and rattled off the stitches of her knit stocking. (This knit stocking was a sort of conversation in itself; and if that was her foundation, you can imagine the rest.) But this particular morning, for some reason, she started to chat. The old man was almost startled. For even if he seemed lifeless, and could give you chills, still he was no stranger to a good word. But he saw that there was no goodness in her words, only calculation. Yet her manner was somehow compelling, it was more than a match for the old man. She was only about forty-five years old, an age at which many women still have tremendous power. And especially (as contradictory as it may seem) when they are usually tight-lipped and unfriendly. Then the rare overture appears like a gleaming point of light, and those who carry sorrow in some corner of their hearts must light up as well. It is the sun of bad conscience, or the sadness of the fearful.

"So," she said, already knitting, "you're all alone now, Mr. Minster? Your wife has died?" He didn't say "Yes" right away, perhaps he didn't say it at all. But at least he looked wordlessly over the edge of his newspaper. "But she suffered for a long time? My God!" Then she returned to knitting. Perhaps she paid a visit to the deceased at the summit of her mountain of knitting. But the old man gave no response to that, either. He knew what it means to be a rich old man. He had married an old woman himself. Of course, back then her hair was still black, and she was barely over fifty. But with that marriage she had begun her decline. From the first day on, and for the next ten years, she was dying. Until her natural time for death had come.

She had been a good wife. Throughout her life, which had followed a straight line from childhood to that final day, she had retained something childlike—not simplemindedness, exactly, but a semblance of simplemindedness; a kind of goodness that one only reluctantly acknowledges as such. That might have been what caused her husband to treat her with increasing cruelty, or even what led him to propose to her in the first place, not out of goodness, but out of a sort of mockery, perhaps.

Yes, she was aging from the first day on. (For what must be begun, must begin at once.) She was aging, even as he seemed to grow more youthful. And from that very first day, she was ashamed of this marriage. Why hadn't she been ashamed of it before? A few days before the wedding she had even bought a dozen bright red carnations for her future window. Oh, if only she hadn't married! Surely she would have remained lively and happy for a long time to come. But in this marriage, she had to sink into sorrowful old age.

They had promptly moved to another city, just as they had planned. Her little house was sold on the last day before the wedding, and with the money she had taken part ownership of a nice tenement building, where she had then lived and died. Ten years. Ten years isn't long? I can assure you that ten years is very long; sometimes even longer than an entire life. It is a cruel pursuit, calamity that comes so late. It claims the dimensions of an existence fully justified. And already she had ceased to smile from joy, smiling only when she was alone now, and only because it had been her habit before. She smiled at her sugar bowl and at her clock, which stood transfigured under a glass dome; she smiled at her yellow canary. But when she died, the bird lay on the sand in its cage as well, it had lived those same ten years along with her. (She had bought this bird at the time of the wedding, too.)

And to put ourselves in the place of the café owner again, we must also ask where the discord in this marriage lay. For she would not accept a natural, harmless explanation of the familiar sort. She rejected almost everything the first time she heard it, only to slowly, discreetly adapt the idea and claim it for her own. At that point there was no use contradicting her, or pointing out that you had said the same yourself, because she was always the first and the last. For her there was nothing but herself and her café. And everything else around was only there to serve these ends. And this, she thought, was the way all others lived their lives as well. And anyone who thought differently only earned her scorn. And even if in some small part of her soul she knew what life was like for others, and that their lives were not like her own, still she gave no credence to this view, because, as mentioned, it contradicted her own principles. This is how it was for her, as she knitted and spoke to the widower. And even though he didn't like all of this, nonetheless he really did stay a while longer than usual. Simply because that was her intention.

Her overture had been pure torture for him. And what had she really asked, then? Almost nothing.

He stood up and left. A day like that is long for an old man. Particularly when he isn't a good old man, but instead an old man like this one. He had no way out, no excuse to escape from this boredom. His young caretaker had diligently deprived him of all such excuses. This was the curse of his spiteful nature, that it had left him all this time for nothing. He walked down the street with the prettiest shop windows. He looked at all the things in them. I can't be sure what he thought as he looked. He walked under the arcades and looked at the weathered paintings, one by one. But more out of elderly absentmindedness than any real interest. Then a parade march summoned him out from beneath an archway. What did he think of music? Nothing. He could actually draw only two distinctions: marches and waltzes. And neither one could ever win him over. The people who cared about such things seemed to him to be chasing a golden goose, bound to it against their will.

And to return to his own life: though from the outside he appeared to be all one color, in fact he was sharply aware, down to the smallest detail, of the pain and sadness he could call forth in those near to him, and of how he himself could be humiliated and made small. For all his own mundaneness, he did not lack an understanding of the mundane.

If he never said hello, but simply sat down at the lunch table—never said hello to that friendly creature (the food, after all, had been cooked in such a spirit), if he never offered his thanks for the fact that his linens were white as blossoms,

71

and gently pressed as a fine gentleman's (as far as class is concerned, he was roughly the equal of a clerk), wasn't her hand bound to slowly, literally weaken? For he ate nothing, enjoyed no pleasure, out of self-inflicted coldness.

How could she continue to work for this man with all her energy as time went by ... After all, every task requires its own source of energy. But he took it away from her, for he didn't live his life with her or even alongside her, he was not even served by her hands, but rather by any old hands. He acted as if she weren't there. He walked right past her. Back then he was only sixty. He was in good health, you could be sure of that. He was like petrified wood. He had paid too dearly for his wife, at least by his own reckoning. He had nothing but disdain for her. But perhaps her own friendliness was to blame for everything. You could see it that way. But she herself, without his noticing, had turned her sorrow and humiliation inward. She humbled herself in her own eyes. For instance, as she silently served her husband, she would say: Now this is your own punishment. Why did you marry this young man anyway, you old fool? (In truth, he was not so young anymore.) But she willfully degraded herself in her own eyes. Had all of that really been necessary? Had the devil himself whispered into her ear that she should marry? Hadn't she had the finest life before? Hadn't she sat at her window as if in a chaise when all her little morning work was done? No one had even disturbed her then, much less aggrieved her. She had had a life like the purest honey.

Thus did she speak to herself as she served her husband. For already on the second day of their married life she had ceased to sit down at the table with him. Think what that must have meant to someone of such harmless character.

But she did not give up entirely. When she saw that he did not respect her as his wife, she made every effort to become a sort of mother to him. But no matter what she did—even if one Sunday, perhaps a holiday or his birthday, she fried crullers in lard for him and set them out on plates with gold trim, served with aromatic coffee in her finest coffeepot, which was normally kept in the glass cabinet—even then she had to clear it all away a short time later, as if it had been nothing but dark bread. And her crullers lost their charm, and the coffee, made in true Arab fashion, might as well have been set before a cliff.

The old man had shut himself off from any sort of goodness, and so over time she lost her spirit, and her hands, too, slowly grew less willing and able. After just a few years she truly could have passed for his mother. And that only further fueled his cruelty. He didn't age anymore until she died. He simply stopped. He turned to petrified wood, as I have said. And when she finally began to grasp this, this and all that there was to grasp, one day her strength left her and she simply remained in bed—as if suddenly she were not just his mother or his grandmother, but a distant ancestor.

The childlike girl, who was even more a child back then, came and cooked her a meal, a porridge, and fed it to her with a spoon. She had suffered a stroke. Soon she stopped speaking altogether. But even before that, she had rarely said more than "Thank you."

But her husband went to the tavern. And in the morning he sat in that café. What had his wife ever done to him? She hadn't married him, he had married her. And besides, he had come into a nice bit of money with the transfer of this profitable tenement building. And they practically lived there alone.

Why did he have to subject her to this slow death? His name was Michael Minster. Was he perhaps the stone house of the devil? Why did he live on, unpunished?

He had not spoken a single warm word to the sick woman. Strangers, one still a child, had cared for her, as if she were not worth the effort of a whole, grown person. It was this child who had placed the candle in her hands as death drew near. But he had shut her eyes in the end.

It was with this guilt that he now sat in the café, walked past the shop windows, took in the landscapes and heard the parade marches and waltzes. Where had God's love been when this man was created. And yet there are people much more callous and evil than he. And many, many more like him, of all varieties. And who can be sure that he himself has not treated his fellow men in such a way at times.

For the ultimate justice does not ask if these times lasted only a moment, or an eternity. Or had men merely invented and created these punishments for themselves? Could a man be his own tribunal, even as others thought him beyond reach? Or was he truly beyond reach? For the childlike girl still comes to the old man's house, still cleans and tidies the rooms, in an impersonal way, with her mind on her own future that is yet to come. She heats the room for him, brings an apple along for herself as a child might, as if it were a ball, and polishes it on her apron to a fiery red. One spring day she even sets freshly picked anemones on the table. But only because she has found so many, and because there are vases there that can hold them, and freshly cleaned rooms in which these flowers can stand.

For these rooms have long since returned from their journey to the land of death. Only once does this thought occur to the girl, and her face betrays foreboding and a general fear. But even then it is only existence itself that has revealingly opened her eyes. For life seems to simply, impassively set down its seasons in this large gray house, be they glowing hot or growing chill. The clock turns inaudibly beneath the glass dome; the old man seems to have reached a point at which he no longer even wants to walk through the streets, or to flip through the newspapers in the little café. In short, he seems to have arrived at the pinnacle of his solitude. But this is in the autumn. The old man has contracted a cold, and he regards his single street from his armchair. She is coming. The café woman is coming, she herself, larger than that room. And in the face of this fate, he simply looks on at first, not knowing if it will pass and leave him only with an endless sense of fear, or if this fate will grab him with its real hands, with its larger-than-life gestures, as if this were the way it was meant to be, as if it were like this for everyone in the world, but then again only for him alone. And yet he had laid out his life for himself, nothing in it had ever happened by chance. He had been a god of his own destiny. And now he felt that he had even come to fear himself. And he began to feel his own bony frame, the way that one suddenly recognizes death. But life is still there too, so seemingly harmless, and it takes hold of him in the most unremarkable forms, for what is there to fear if that café woman comes to visit—that plump woman, full of cares in her own way, but also mighty—if she comes to ask after his well-being? For it really has been too long since he was in her little shop, that old man there.

Strawberries

And the same thing returns again and again, as if there were only one life in great-grandmother, grandmother, mother, in grandfather, father, and children.

Oh how bright it would be in us if one day we could work this off, if we could begin ...

When the strawberries ripen in the woods and gardens and spread their many-colored fragrance along the currents of the air, when we feel childhood and the morning of a mother, of the many working people all around us in the world, the city with its greening gardens surging like waves around its walls, when we feel how even all the voiceless things are owners and bearers of life when the time is right, then we grow more confident, more comforting, and not for nothing. We are young ourselves, and we share in the beauty of a June day, we are deep within it like a blackbird's song. But because we can have all this without sharing in the effort of existence, because we are not prepared to fall from the air like birds, because we need a shelter all the same, and cannot merely view the earth from above like a relief, there is danger even in such beauty. Suddenly we are no longer there as people for the people around us, the path of our fate has vanished like a dead man's ... We live outside of our being, and one day we are found like a plant, slowly rotting into the earth.

Then clarity must help us, if it comes at the right time, that clarity that many call love, the evergreen landscape of our own hearts.

The strawberries were ripening under their dark-haired leaves; it brought to mind an old picture in our house, with its view from the palace and the palace garden of the chaste Susanna at her bath …

There were hands that grew lecherous at the sight, like those two old men. They were prepared to risk dishonor in the eyes of the whole world: and yet they did it …

But when the one who is defiled is a garden, then only the deep blue June sky is the judge, and only the seemingly silent road is the world, the gardens with their gray stone enclosures, with their silver-green shrubbery, with the arabesques of shadows on the gray faces of the houses.

A narrow garden wrapped around the house; the type of garden little people keep, only there to be looked at. But not just by those passing in the street outside; inside, too, bright blossoms bore ripening pears, though it was hard to say for whom.

First of all, there was the man who owned the house and garden, but he didn't live in the house or in the garden, he lived up on the mountain, and no one had ever seen him harvesting his fruit. And when he was working there during the day—for the house in which we lived was just his factory building— when he looked down from his window, everything jumped: his tenants' children and the butterflies and the butterflies' shadows and a bird that swooped down with a chirp to catch a small caterpillar. And the pears and red currants were not yet ripe. And between the bright days there was always a night, and no one knew if it was the birds or the unguarded minds of children that so quickly caught sight of the yellow and red colors and shapes amidst the green foliage, and saw the garden only in its berries. Or was it a thief who came in the night; an outright thief, which is just what he wished to be called, for what would have become of him if someone had recognized him and called him by his proper name? No, no one wanted to catch a man like that. They would much rather strew a bit of salt on the little birds' tails during the day.

Those were the thoughts of the factory owner and boss as he looked out the window at the garden before the harvest, and his thoughts were so mild that he was content with them.

Yet it's easy to be benevolent on a whim like that. Such a whim won't take you at your word. You can go home from work to a cozy table feeling pleased with yourself for being a just man. Indeed, it seems that such a good deed of omission, lying out in the sun like an ostrich egg, has a way of inspiring particular confidence. You laugh in silence. The whole world turns to gold when you touch it.

But outside the scent is drifting on the air. It wafts through the rooms, across the empty platters arranged on the credenzas, it hides in a bouquet of flowers. But perhaps it finds a little bunch of strawberries in a glass jar and collects around them, growing into a large, invisible, aromatic bouquet.

Oh, if there were angels that lived on fruit alone, their arms folded over their breasts, they would eat the ripe fruits from the stalk where they hung and waited, angels whose incense would be the fragrance of flowers and fruits.

But nowhere is this the case, this kiss must remain in the realm of the unfulfilled.

In the northward-facing rooms, the day ascended only gradually to its peak. The shadow of the foliage still fell heavily into the sitting room, colliding with it. The lightest things were the real sounds, the canary hopping up and down, up to its perch and then down to the sand and then up to its perch again. And the clock, always the clock; but the clock again, with its numbered hours that only mattered in the morning and around midday, pounded like the pulse in a mother's freshly washed hand, resting for a moment in her lap. When such a room has been aired out and freshly made up by a mother, it is as if a child were lying there in a cradle. Everything hums at this early hour.

The curtains, though, hang motionless in their bluish folds. The narcissus is reflected in the windowpane. The loving look that the mother cast back on the room before she dutifully left, returning its greeting, hangs in the air.

And the shouts that filter in from the street have no place here: nor does the wagon that inscribes the road outside with its slow roll. That is a script of its own. These fully written tablets are always held up for the room to see. But the room does not see them. The day inside has its own currency.

Then, I can't remember, drummers and pipers passed by, suddenly all the windows were open, and someone who was already making his way again down the steps and through the corridors called out, recollecting his happiness: "Oh, strawberries!"

Yes, their scent was there, and the silence, too, it was precious ...

We children came home. We were small and still unfamiliar in that street. Only the nearest neighbors knew what clothes we wore, what we ate from day to day, how our mother was ... Those who lived further down the road only knew our name, they tried it out on each of us, the way people call young animals to them, which then go on their way once they see that this is not their master.

So we, more knowing even than older people and yet less real than anything, gradually made our way home that day. We had brought the garden with us, so to speak. There was space for it in this big, wide parlor. And the room had been alone long enough. The sun-circled strawberries were firmly in our minds. It was as if someone had held them before our eyes. Not scattered about, as we see them today and tomorrow, but the way that only the birds surely see them, with their berry-round eyes.

But we weren't just thinking about the fenced-in garden with the little rose bushes, with the wreaths of strawberries, with the fragrance of chestnut blossoms. The street itself was on our minds. We played there with our hands even while they lay waiting on the tables, as children's hands will before lunch. We didn't speak. The gold of the midday sun called for silence. But our mother came. The narcissus flowers were ruffled by the sudden draft, the curtains floated up in their white house dress. Now we could speak and eat. Perhaps it was nothing but hunger and weariness ... To be sure, we were hungry and weary, but still we had no desire to speak and eat. It was a true witching hour around midday. Even mother's face didn't seem to be there. It was still over the stove.

Not a single sweet word was to be found there, and it could have been just an everyday word—we felt no need at all to please each other, we simply loved each other—but even those daily words could not be found.

It's a strange thing about human thoughts. If I told someone this story, he would probably have trouble saying at this point what it was about, since nothing had been thought yet, nothing had been done. It had only been felt: just down the street, where the houses ended, was the small strawberry garden, pierced through by thousands of the sun's trembling arrows. And its ripe blood seemed to be measured in hours. And its leaves offered drowsy cover. The fragrance was flowing. We knew: one minute we would smell the chestnut flowers with bees humming around them, the next a round bed of narcissus, the next the gentle scent of pansies. But when the strawberries floated over to us again, this meal seemed bleak and burdensome, far from inviting; we wanted to stand up and go.

On workdays there was no dessert for us. And so our proper, homely meal was no match for this June day. We stood as if caught in a small cage of spring and summer.

And our mother, young and grown at once, had firmly closed her heart to all those fenced-in gardens. Her face offered no intercession. Particularly where the narrow garden around our own white house was concerned, she thought that it fell outside the realm of her experience, and so she advised us to play in the streets and gardens further along. After all, the small garden door might suddenly give way. Who knew the magic of its summer pleasure ...

Perhaps you will argue that the three of us had never learned to go without. But what does it mean to go without—assuming that we really couldn't do it—if not to take pleasure in looking at things. We returned from our trips to market feeling sated, and often we hadn't bought a single bouquet, a single basket of early cherries. And the treasure chest of our minds was wide open. But the little mirror inside that chest had only to reflect the ground; it showed the stand piled high with fruit and vegetables. But we felt how that world, like jewelry and old music, was transformed and passed over into us.

But the strawberry garden did not want to be transformed. It was the garden of all gardens; no one's sweat and toil, no one's property, and yet closed off, seemingly given over to itself. It was basically only a small front garden that looked down onto a round plaza and the broad street below, but it emerged powerfully from the earth: it had already conquered our hearts. From that moment on, all the other things no longer worked for us.

But what that can mean for a child, to be without a world …

Meanwhile we still played in the sand in the park, as mother had told us to do. Our small wooden wagon was loaded with stones. There were stones everywhere. Stones in colors and forms more varied than thoughts. There seemed to be a stone for every stroke of fancy, for every grasp. But they were hard nonetheless, stones through and through. In the end that drove us away from that place. This human language of renunciation and utter solitude was strange and almost eerie for us children.

We rose and went up the street, our hands resting gently on the wagon's steering rod. We went in a hurry. It seemed that no one saw us. We went around the village fountain beneath the lindens, we went around each tree. Finally we sang a little May song, but quietly, as if no one should hear it, in the blindness of the sun. We were alone; we were small, and that offered us cover, made us almost invisible. We stood mutely before the iron bars of the front garden, while time after time went by. We saw nothing. The leaves were rough and jagged, but then a strawberry caught our eye, as if unexpectedly. But then a hand was already on the latch of the small gate. And the wagon followed. And we sat at the edge of the bushes and looked under the leaves and reached under the leaves. And the fruit was sweet, at the height of its sweetness. The berries fell into our hands as soon as we touched those clusters. And so many ... We looked down at our hands: we held four of our hands together, small hands, and their lines, like the lines of our faces, had barely begun to form.

Then we looked at the little wagon. And we found that gravel belonged with gravel, so we emptied it out.

And then, with effusive eagerness, we covered the empty bottom of the wagon with leaves. And there was one strawberry and then another and soon it was red upon red. And when we were tired and squatting like little hares, unable to continue, late afternoon had already come to the world outside. The evening street was clear upon clear. Every door was a mouth, every window a face, and all at once we felt that all the gardens were open to us. Suddenly we were afraid. We were still alone. Then we rose, and the little wagon followed, what else could it have done ... We guarded it carefully against tipping over. I can still remember the way that someone looked down at us from a closed window, astonished and curious. But it was unthinkable that the strawberries did not belong to us, if we were pulling them home so openly in our wagon. We could see that in the person's face. But we were like thieves in the night, our appearance betrayed nothing. Even if someone had suddenly asked us: "Who are you, and what have you done here," it could not have startled us out of our dream-sure wakefulness. We had truly forgotten ourselves, were no longer real. Our knowledge was no knowledge at all. So we returned home.

We were happy to find that there was no one in the rooms, and we could fill the empty platters on the credenzas. The evening sun was shining. The bird was ruffling itself in the water. The clock began to chime. It passed. We didn't count its strokes. We, too, had left the room. I don't remember anymore if we stood with the maid in her freshly pressed apron as she dangerously waved the clothes iron, if we slid down the banister, or joined one of the animated evening games that the children played in the alley outside. But in the end we forgot, and became like the others.

And we returned home so untroubled and refreshed that it must have been a joy.

Not a breath reminded us of what had happened. Everything was just as usual, and we sat in our usual places.

But what shock, what silent shock: no soup was served, no vegetables, not even a piece of bread for each of us, but only three plates full of strawberries. We knew them, we knew them well. And each of us ate, bent over, doing our solemn duty. We didn't look at each other's hands, nor at each other's faces. Even our mother spoke not a word, but simply ate her portion along with us. No accusation, no sharp "You'd better be full now!" which we had truly earned; no "If and but ..."

The room now smelled as if it truly held a garden ... Our hands were red, since there were no spoons on the table, and none of us had been bold enough to fetch them.

But there was also no judgment, hidden and waiting some-where. With this meal, everything seemed to be atoned for. The night was there, like a large, soft field of pansies. We went to sleep there, tired and without a thought.

And mother was mother and children remained children, mercifully spared.

The Hot Air Balloon

It was a very sunny day when the hot air balloon was to take flight. It didn't even look foolish to stretch your arms out as if to touch it; sometimes the whole world appears to be painted on porcelain, right down to the dangerous cracks.—

The green was already showing on all of the trees and shrubs, but only at the very tips—as if a green hand had brushed over them—and Easter wasn't far off anymore, such thoughts could cross one's mind.

It had to be a very bright and windless day for the balloon to take off. I don't know if the others cared, the important people with their children and their servants. But it mattered quite a bit to our mother; she thought everyone should be able to go along to the launch. Just imagine climbing up with that captive air, higher than all the mountains where the gentians bloom, above the edelweiss. My God! it was certainly dangerous. Perhaps even sinful, she reflected. And all at once the earth seemed to grow dark. It was certainly dangerous ... What if the balloon were stranded over the sea, forever and ever, until its pilot died of grief and fell down like a little rag, alone, with the balloon still hanging in the sky ... Children certainly believe that it is possible to see everything beyond death. There is a place inside them that is not like a picture just drawn on paper. If we could hold onto that love that feels so alive in childhood, we would be the truest sort of magicians. We would learn: Never to die. A sound would still carry over, across the waters of death, and whoever approached the shore and gazed across would see only water lilies blooming. That was how we thought of the balloon. We thought of it with our Sunday clothes and with our arms and with our faces.

The voices reminded us of it, and so did the whole wide Sunday world. People were streaming along the road to the church. A boy, small like us, was drumming in front of the weighmaster's little house, shouting and stamping in such a way that his knees knocked against the skin of the drum. It was an awful business. He wasn't going to the sports field to see the hot air balloon. He had a giant drum just like that all to himself. He drummed for his street, for his father, for everyone who wasn't out there sparkling in the sun. But his father sat at the window. He saw us and we saw him, and he saw his child and we saw the boy. And we heard him too. But the weighmaster lived behind deaf windows. The world is a giant mirror, and suddenly we find ourselves face to face with one another, unable to turn away. "That man," our mother said, "is always sitting there inside his house." If he had suddenly been transformed into a wooden post, the post where horses were hitched in front of the giant scale, the shock would have been no greater. "Always"—that word has made globetrotters of more than a few. We felt this in the horror that the word provoked in us. Ah, there are a thousand ways to measure one's fate. And with justice. This much has been provided for us. We always want to be certain where each step comes from, where it is going. And even the lightest footfall leaves its trace.

Then a bird's call suddenly broke into these thoughts, dispersing them. We continued on our way. Our dresses were almost scorching from the midday heat, and it was too early for that. But those afternoon hours, those many sunny hours, seemed to have turned once and for all into a single hour, so that a boy could walk through his garden in shirtsleeves in the winter. And so it is. We can risk anything; we hold our senses overhead like a burning mirror. And almost Easter ... Already it seemed we had seen more flowers than in all the previous years. Liverworts and daisies and snowdrops and violets, all those little short-stemmed plants. Flowers that would never grow as high as the rest of the meadow, where they now stood alone, the very first. We thought of the hot air balloon again, and hurried along. We were close to the launch field. But there were fewer and fewer people on the road, and none were coming toward us, as if there were no one at all where we were going. We were somewhat disconcerted. It was not a pleasant feeling. We'd thought we wouldn't see a single tavern here that wasn't lively, packed full of people too far off to recognize, with streamers blowing in the air, waving to us down the mountain.

"We're there now," someone said with a sigh of relief. And more and more of us repeated it. We hadn't known that there were taverns that stood empty, their flags hoisted every day, in the rain and at night and late into the autumn, until they faded with the first snowflakes and had to be taken down, stiff with cold. But we could already sense this and fear it, without having ever experienced it. That Sunday flower of faces that should have been milling about could not be seen from afar, either. But all of a sudden, in the space between two houses, we saw the sports field spread out, stretching in all directions. And there, bound to the earth with ropes, small against the unattainable sky, was the hot air balloon. And all around the hot air balloon stood a pack of children, the kind who seem to live on the sports field all summer, to live from watching. Women who regretted having made this endless trip waited behind them, prayer books held in their impatient hands. And behind them stood a man who was turning on his heel as if he could do it all much better. Aside from him there was another father, a craftsman—you could tell that just by looking at him—he was like carnations that refuse to bloom, set in the sun of a low window. He looked on: maybe he would buy his children a balloon one day, too; just a small one, though, a red one. But this balloon was made of fabric that shone like silk. "Gray belongs in the blue," it seemed to say. Each color added to the other. But the blue of the sky would tremble like fire if you stared at it too long. In light of all this, we might have forgotten the hot air balloon, perhaps it was already sailing far, far away, already vanished and nearing the gentians that spread out like a sky beneath it, its own breeze grazing the edelweiss and the spires of the high cities.

Mother gave me her parasol to hold. She wanted to take out her money, I saw that it was fifty centimes. That was a lot. Beggars usually received three centimes for a piece of bread, circus riders ten centimes. A small, plump, gray-haired woman was collecting the money. This woman was distressed, it went without saying, for who doesn't know that feeling, when so few people come out for such a spectacle; no people at all, you could say, since the few who were there turned away when they saw the collection plate, so that in the end the sum was so small that it could no longer even be divided. She was no acrobat in a leotard doing head-first dives. Even the children, her grandchildren, stood by themselves, along that line so carefully drawn by hardship. They stood looking out at the wide plain, not up at the sky as we did, the sky seemed to be spoiled for them. So that was the tavern with the flag … They looked frozen, too, like people who have had to wait and watch for a long time. As if in a solemn children's game we had come up to them and asked outright: "Are you the tavern?" and they had shaken their heads violently, so that everyone could see that they meant "no." They were nothing but their own hardship, like a garden on the north slope: the red turned to pink, the blue to light blue, the yellow just a hint of gold. We should have given them ten francs, ten francs, without a second thought. These were people who had to live from one day to the next, who thought back on the suffering that they had survived as if remembering days of good fortune that held the promise of a long life. It was enough to make you shudder. It didn't matter if you had seen it, if you had witnessed it. The sight of these people, small and inexperienced, grown old in their poverty, was almost too much to be believed. "But wait," a voice was calling somewhere, "there are no age differences, there is no miserliness, no privation." It was as if a strong man had lifted his heavy barbells into the air, his golden chest glistening against the sky, the way that this mean feat was placed before our eyes, to make our charity seem like a bargain. We looked down at the ground, ashamed of our insignificance, which was more powerful than anything, otherwise that man would have gotten the better of us. But for now there was still ground beneath us, no fairy tale and no truth could make us forget that. This great compassion, when does it come to dwell in us? We don't have it in childhood, we don't have it in the strength of our youth, perhaps we don't even have it in old age. To give is a simple thing. Perhaps generosity is found elsewhere as well, in patience, perhaps even in hardship, when it has not yet taken hold of us and transformed us. Hardship is a razor-sharp science: we will treat of it no more. I don't believe that the fifty centimes were a paltry sum to the grandmother, although her gray, everyday eyes made no reply. Sometimes one person must take the place of the many who did not come or did not pay. They knew, too. There had been a brief notice in the daily paper, something like: "Weather permitting, an acrobat hanging from a hot air balloon will perform this Sunday. All are invited to attend." Date, time, and location.

And now the sphere was slowly moving. We saw his children loosening the ropes. And the man himself, like an empty town square where several roads suddenly meet, adjusted his leather belt, with which—you never know, perhaps out of weariness—he might later tie himself to his trapeze, high above in the open air. He checked one last time if his belt was snug, blew a kiss, like a half moon in the afternoon sky, swung himself up onto the trapeze when it had reached the height of his head, and ascended further and further into the heavens. His daring swings were spectacular. Once we saw him outside the trapeze, both legs extended straight into the air, only holding on with his left hand. We looked on. In our hands (we felt) we held something that wasn't there. We wanted to come to his aid, because up there in the air … The acrobat beneath the hot air balloon … How far away he must be even at that moment … How long an hour must feel to him … The day was gentle and mild. But we, like lizards, blinking, slipped quickly back under our rocks.

The Christmas Visit

A bove the strawberry garden, on the second story, worked
a clerk who had once been a typesetter. Our mother told
us that in an earnest tone. "He had such respect for his work
that you had to admire him, even if they were all the same letters in all the same places where any other typesetter would
have put them. We're going to go pay him a visit during the
Christmas holidays." And that was important to us, and a short
time later we festively took the little letter that announced our
visit. And it wasn't just important to us because it was a visit.
No, as simple, ordinary children, we were all the more able to
grasp the significance of this in our minds, to glimpse the visit's
meaning with the clarity and truth that lay hidden within it.

Even the simple fact that the man lived on the other side
of the hill, that he had the courage to draw his own breath
between what was newly created and what was still evolving,
this fact alone was enough to excite our minds, and so we entered his house upright and alert.

He greeted us himself. He came toward us with just the
brisk, decisive stride that we had anticipated. His wife came.
His children stood waiting in the doorways of the spacious
corridor until they were called. "This is our house," they said

gracefully, "and this here is Gretchen." They took our coats. And then came the little procession to the Christmas parlor. And what a room it was! If we had been alone, we certainly would have taken a step back. There was a bird singing in there, as secret and sparkling as if he were sitting in the branches outside. And even though we had brought our unfamiliar, wide-eyed presence with us into the room, the minutes kept running ripe and clear, bringing moisture to what would otherwise have dried up, to what should not be forgotten. And the festivity began there, too—unruffled, it began just where it always did, at the small sewing table, as if in person, humble and plain. Since it was Sunday, and there was no work to be done, this festive spirit was weaving together hundreds and hundreds of rings of sunlight, and taking them apart again. But then came the table, courting us with its own scents. The honey cakes and the cinnamon stars, the many sorts of butter cookies, they were all prepared to trade with one another, or even to be given as gifts if the occasion allowed. Meanwhile they kept growing sweeter and crisper, believing that all of this came from the Christmas tree. But the tree, too, had retained the round shape measured out for it by the sun, at once a tree of the forest and a Christmas tree. But I don't recall how it was decorated. Only that I liked it. I've forgotten, too, what gifts lay on the white-and-blue-stitched cloth. But they must have been chosen with great care, with the care of the three hundred and sixty-five days of the year. When we had had our fill of looking and tasting, a little Christmas carol began, like a small manger set into the moss. And the two children sang of the news from heaven, echoing their parents' voices with such joy that one had to listen and smile. The children's interwoven melodies—like a soaring proclamation—were gifts, too, and we gathered the words from their mouths.

Then we were called into the living room; there I noticed a doll's cradle. But the boy had spread out an atlas where you could see the entire world; how the land suddenly stuck its tongue out into the sea. With joyful eyes the boy wandered into that world. Understanding is love. It is nothing in itself, though it may be fully present in a person; it only continues naturally on and on. And whatever may inspire it or fulfill it is fully absorbed in our body and mind: this way we do not bump up against the pointy outcroppings of others. And so the atlas was truly a gift. But it was folded up and put away. Then came the cups and the tall coffeepot and the crystal sugar bowl, and Christmas was there in yet another form. The whipped cream—which they called *Niedl*—was truly tempting, but it also lent a formal air to this festive occasion. Who wouldn't have wanted to have those lovely gifts come to visit once a year, on flowery damask! And with such fine manners, such propriety and reserve, that the little silver spoon seemed to bow, before it was lifted with delight. And the conversation echoed this conviction of the goodness, the soundness of all those things not experienced firsthand, and the rightness of each person. This was the same reverence as at the typesetting tray. A child could understand that. It was clear as water, supple and free of any unwelcome aftertaste, but also hard and steady like the water that wears away much harder stones. Of course we children rarely had the chance to pose a question, but our ears were always intent on the conversation.

Finally we rose and looked at the St. Barbara's branch blooming in the window. It was such a perfectly wintry thing to bring these tiny pink buds into bloom, encircled by their pointy side leaves. And the hyacinths, which shot their white roots into the water like flames. They had been placed a way off because of their strong fragrance. But they pulled even further away of their own accord. All of their hyacinth air slipped out through the cracks in the windows and the gaps in the house. It left us at a loss. Only the flower remained. But outside, too, it was a flowery evening, and the room itself seemed slowly to have pulled away. Not long ago it had been right in the middle, as we ate the *Niedl* and the torte … We looked back, disconcerted. The tablecloths were gone now. A small, plain jardiniere stood on the table. A door opened quietly, and a boy's voice sang out invitingly: "Father, the magic lantern is ready." Oh, children, children had everything they wanted here. We leapt up and took our places, grateful and ready, in the roomy entrance hall. We hadn't even noticed its other purpose as we entered. "Children, you have to move in further," said the man, and lifted Gretchen together with her chair into the even darker background. And then we heard the glass plates slowly begin to turn. And we were inside, in the world of the pictures and the colors. Our own movements were transformed into fitful, angular advances, or cautious retreats. The red was like walking in the hottest sun, holding mother's hand, eyes closed. Red was also the furthest, most extreme cold: there the moon became the sun. But the sun itself had lost its power. Blue was the color of the water. And yellow, since time immemorial, had been the color of a thousand dandelions. That was the emblem of this color. A mill wheel began to turn. A hammer pounded on its anvil. Seasons emerged as if out of books, with elves and dwarves. Summer was piled high on wobbling wagons returning to town, a sight that inspired confidence. And there was winter. Children rode sleds into the white of the screen and disappeared. It was strange, almost upsetting.

The whole thing didn't last any longer than it takes a Sunday guest to drink his little glass of liqueur in the park in town below, or a teetotaler to preach his devout praise of abstinence in the large gymnasium. We stood up, greatly enriched but slightly diminished, as is always the case when something ends so suddenly. After all, the magic lantern was brand new, so it didn't have so many slides. It was also possible that we, with our senses so occupied, had been unable to retain everything. And since this lovely afternoon was drawing to an end, it was the natural time to part. They brought two pastries from the Christmas parlor, ladies with raisin eyes for us to take home with us. And they fetched our coats and helped us into them as carefully as if we had been their own children. We bid farewell to each and all, almost a bit wistfully. Then the door was closed. Then we were on the steps, then in the snow on the street. The four faces followed us part of the way ...

How well joy has equipped us, endowing us with hearing, sight, and taste, indeed, with basic things, simple, pure life, traveling a path that it must travel anyhow. And yet joy is like a flowering tree, or like winter twigs covered in snow, or like the bare contours of late autumn. It does with us what it will, indeed, many things ...

Retold ...

The morning sun was shining on the flowers. In the dewy air a young bird was contentedly fluffing its feathers. In the room inside, the light was reflecting like golden water.

A bouquet stood proudly on the table. The floor with its fantastical inlays, the chairs with their pattern like a purely drawn breath, even the small mementos in the glass case were filled with an ardent hardworking spirit, and they shone from within.

Once a young girl entered and looked around. "How nice it is, when a room is so peaceful that you only have to stand in the doorway to have a rest," she thought, and went back to her work.

On the gravel outside, everything was moving at a slow trot. A steady old voice was calling the hens together. The pigeons flew to the windowsill; a turkey let out its rolling tones. You could hear the birds pecking, the grains falling, and so you knew about the earthenware bowl without even having seen it.

Everything looked joyful, still eagerly bound up in blooming. Even the blind old woman calling and feeding the hens outside was no exception. She knew the mountains. Those paths were still under her feet, even here in her new home.

Sometimes she would sing psalms, or recall the names of rare stones, or circle around the house with her walking stick. Today she had also shelled countless fruits of the garden, and set the table there herself.

And the young girl kept bringing out porcelain or a wrapped-up set of silverware. The old woman even set the glasses just where they belonged.

Eventually she went inside, too. Now nothing seemed to be lacking. It was time to give in to that joy. For an hour it was silent. It seemed as if there were no one at all in the house. And the maid stood upstairs in her attic room in front of her tiny mirror and tried on her new starched apron from Christmas. Then she quickly neatened her bureau, which had to double as a table in a little nook like that, straightened the chair, and opened the window again. You could never know ... And this room, too, was left alone again. And around that same time the others were leaving their houses, too, nicely done up in bonnets that shaded their eyes or in finely pressed summer dresses, in gray, in black, in ivory. But if you expected cheerful people to have cheerful faces, you'd be wrong. Their silent faces wear such solemn expressions that you could almost think they were sad. They have the thoughtful, expectant look of the man who has done everything, and is prepared for what is to come.

Still, it's true that the conscience of this house was not entirely clear. To be sure, it stood there sparkling inside and out, polished to a shine like a goblet. And a snow-white goose had been plucked, and the poetry of the kitchen had eventually transformed this goose, along with the young pea pods and the other first fruits of the garden, into a pâté that all the guests would crave. It was meant to look like a small, casual, gentlemen's breakfast, but to taste more delicious than any midday meal. It should all be gone within the hour, that feast that had taken a day to prepare. For even what was already clean, spotlessly clean each and every day, had been taken up again as if it were dusty and rusted: so that finally brass shone like fire, and silver like fathomless glass. And at the end? Ah, the end of such a breakfast is truly one of the most enduring memories; people cherish it more than we think.

We should make nothing of the fact that one person's face wears a lost expression, that another looks severely harsh, that a third can be recognized at once by his clumsy gait, a fourth by his voice, which is higher than anything you might compare it to, and seems to come out of the ground like the voice of a cricket. We can't just go and say: "I don't want to put in too much effort for this man. Much less for that one." At bottom, everyone is worth endless effort, and that goes for us as well as for them. And that the things themselves should finally attain their earthly clarity ... As the sound of the bell seems to long for the striking of the hour, so every house longs for its own festive time.

But a small and wicked, malicious pleasure was lying in wait. It was already reflected large and small in the garden globes. But whenever someone turned around to find it in reality, it would laugh, saying over and over: "I'm not there ..."

"Certainly," said the venerable, overly stern matron, who was now sitting at a slight distance from the table, but still facing it, "the bundt cake that you all wanted to bake would have been foolish and out of place. Just because we live in the country, you think we should have a peasant cake on the table ... even a blind man can see that that's foolish." The sentence took on enormous weight, silence ensued, although someone ought to have replied. The puritanical clarity of this mountain woman, who kept her senses sharp with herbs and stones, truly admitted of no retort.

You couldn't make anything up when she was around. You most certainly couldn't defend needless or foolhardy things to her. And what was even worse, though luckily it happened only rarely: with a silent nod to her blindness, people would simply do what they pleased, unseen.

But she noticed when there was an extra stranger seated at the table, even if he had never spoken and hardly moved. She noticed it without letting on. She knew it must be difficult to carry on at such great length. And she noticed, too, when others were merely preoccupied in their thoughts. And in her straightforward way, she was like a small burning mirror. Whatever this mirror was trained on, whether a person or a thing, it would begin to burn in anguished honesty.

It didn't help that the guests came: that they took the measure of this limitless warmth, this attentive joy that people feel for each other in those moments, when their only regret is that they can't do more for each other. It didn't help that this was a moment when they could truly see; that each person had his own sense of proportion, and could sense that the others did as well: still the petty eyes kept searching in silence for something else. What would it have mattered if they wanted to have a piece of cake to go with their last sip of wine. But the old woman hadn't let them bake the bundt cake, she wouldn't hear of it. Nevertheless, it was a relief to realize that no one was really thinking of anything besides what was already there. They nodded back and forth to each other, dug deep into the pâté, and thought as they looked around the garden that this was the most beautiful place on earth! The lady of the house had disappeared, the maid and the young girl had carried the platters back into the house, and white rolls were lying here and there alongside the glasses.

One of the gentlemen stood up, his gray top hat wobbling over everyone. A bit hunched over, he began to speak; like a young boy slowly pulling in the string and winding it back up to bring his kite down from the sky. "My God," he said, "I feel that the world is beautiful, and that this beauty is not only on the outside, but that it comes from the heart as well. Let's have a good drink, gentlemen, to the health of the hale old mother, and to the health of the lady of the house." The lady of the house was already standing in the doorway, her face flushed. In her hands she held a platter with a bundt cake on a large stiff doily. Her hands were tied, so to speak, she couldn't raise a glass and take a small, satisfying sip to express her thanks. Instead, she gave the bundt cake a happy little shake, and when she got to the table she began to cut it, letting that take the place of words.

But then, like a small, curled dragon, the lie came crawling out of the cake. It had been purchased at the last minute from the baker, and from the outside it looked just like every other bundt cake in the world. As for the astonishment that it produced, you could simply accept it in silence, just as she had done; but you could not simply accept the candid truth that was its real core.

A trusting person, however, of all people, would like to pull off an elegant lie someday, like this lie brought in from outside. All the more when that lie is unspoken … But the cake spoke, it was lemon yellow inside, through and through. The knife stuck fast in it, it couldn't find the way in or out. And now no one could deny that it came from the baker. That was no praise at all for a country mother.

Now she stood there, and she wouldn't even let the maid take that miserable saffron cake from her hands. No, it seemed that she was serving it out quite properly, quite completely, until finally the last crumb had disappeared under the matron's fine smile.

The fountain splashed and played its royal game with the little golden ball. A bird sent its song into the air, so that everyone looked and was caught up in the words of this language.

But then the time was almost at an end again, this good hour. The young girl came to the table with a little basket on her arm, bringing each of the guests one of the roses or buds that grew in the garden. Her smile was hidden, like the fragrance of the flowers. And each person took the flower in his own way, and depending on the sort, put it on his hat or in a buttonhole, or held it by the very end of its stem, as if it could easily wilt. And all of them, young and old, at once embarrassed and amused by this adornment, made their way back to the station, garrulous with wine.

The Hunchback

The living room was alone again. There was only an old maid passing through to shut the windows. You could think of it as any time of year you pleased, from March to September. The light was a rainy rose color. The streets must have been damp. The roofs were, in any case. The sky settled there like the pigeons that strutted across those roofs, holding their breasts puffed out before them. They almost seemed to be there in that room.

But mostly there were only bird cages, not an unusual sight in the home of a hunchback, they were mounted on the walls beside the windows, at just the right height to be seen by someone crouched over his work. But the two occupants, each in his own cage, were covered with a small green cloth. They sang, in turn or in unison. They were bullfinches, and they had forgotten their songs, as they did each year during molting season. And the covering might have been meant to distract them from all thoughts of spring, and to reacquaint them with those well-practiced melodies. Their tongues had been loosened, and one of them sang as if it were a bubbling spring, and had only just thought to sing those songs men often wrote to accompany its flowing notes. So it poured forth, as if the song had recollected itself again. Then all was silent for a while, and you could only speculate that the singer was enjoying a little bunch of lettuce, and his neighbor had dipped his feathered head into a water bath; for joy is to be shared on earth. And the room trembled and wobbled a bit, so alone, delicate as a young girl …

There wasn't a mirror in the room—oh, yes, on the door, in a darkish spot; and in it you could glimpse a Christ child under a glass dome. Then the singing began again, like the voice of a young girl in church. God, what a room that was. How the sun ripened there, too. The sofa had spread out its flower garden. There was an order there, too, it felt like early spring. And some people are like that all the time. They always have ears for that first season of their soul. But it would be unjust indeed to deny them their sentiments. It is the pure melody of their hearts, it is their unclouded truth. In the face of that, all preaching falls away, in the end they know more than we do. Above all, they have a real home. What was there, was breathing like the hundred-year-old ivy of a garden. It might be sentimental, but it was sacred, too. Is it even possible to draw such a distinction without being truly heartless? Can we even possibly enter the mind of a thoroughly uneducated person? The way that he has constructed the world for himself out of inherited customs and laws discovered on his own … But despite the apparent risk of growing caught in this cocoon, there was a sobriety there, too. There was order there, as I have said. And cleanliness, too, its natural consequence. There was an old writing desk, you could see that it was used for calculations. And there was another corner that looked like a workshop. Violins were hanging there, made for angels, never touched by a finger, these instruments may have been more than precious; there were unfinished violins hanging there, violin necks with fingerboards and violins without backs. You could gaze into the mystery of the violin. Down from the wall came a sound like the song in a dream. You not only saw it, you felt it: this was the workshop of a violin maker.

Then a clock that had been ticking unnoticed, soft as velvet, began to strike its melody, three times. And as if the bird had found its song again in those strokes, or as if there were no bird at all in the room, but only an ancient clock that played a song to mark the hour, the room was singing again, a patient, maidenly folk song.

And now the scents were stirring, too. It mostly smelled like wood. The violins smelled like the wood of refined trees. Was there a birch among them, that tree that yields healing water when tapped with a pipe? I didn't know, I almost doubted it, I know nothing about violin making. But I liked the thought that this birch was such a melodic tree ...

So here, too, in this craftsman's pious, almost childlike world, large things were squeezed small enough to grasp, while small things were made inconceivably large, for these trees had been made into violins, and violins into trees.

A single photograph hung above the small workbench, a picture of a child. The little hunchback standing next to his mother. His mother sat there with the look of someone who does something out of pride, but almost dies of shame in the process. And the son, the child? Oh, we don't need to describe him. He had a mother, and so he was in good hands. He rested his own hand on her shoulder, with one foot forward (he was wearing long pants). It must have been a memento of his first communion, this little picture. And on the other side of the room, above the baby Jesus in the glass dome, another, crucified Christ hung on the wall. His rib cage protruded, and his arms stood out from the cross, revealing his shoulder blades so clearly that he, too, appeared to have been a hunchback, this God incarnate. Who could have put that crucifix there so casually? And in just that spot? For it was reflected in the iridescent shimmer of the glass dome, so sharply that it seemed to shatter the dome into a thousand shards, and to destroy the tender, comely little waxen Jesus child. It was truly a cause for concern. You could even start to wonder if the nail was fixed firmly in the wall.

And even if the son was an orphan now, all this was his home, the steadfast home of this one man. The maid, who had left me alone the whole time while I waited (the violin maker would be back in half an hour), came in and talked to me. It was a surly sort of chitchat, but it told me all that mattered: it told me what might be in one of the drawers, in writing or in a picture, though I never would have looked without permission.

She asked if I was going to the circus, too. This circus, which seemed to have stretched the tent of its excitement over the whole town. Ever since, you could hear the lions roaring, and elephants walked down the street in broad daylight, almost alone.

I was convinced that these animals wouldn't hurt the slightest creature, much less us people. But the surly maid couldn't believe that … If you were that big, with feet and teeth like that. She looked at me disparagingly … Somehow I had transgressed against this servant's point of view by belittling the mental faculties of that animal—for that's what she thought I had done. "I'm not going to the circus," she added at once, by way of explanation. God knows what else lay buried in that conversation. "I'm not, but my master Jakob is." But now, all at once, she fell silent. For now everything was there on the surface, so that even her awkward silence spoke.

An entire life spent with one person is everything. She had held this hunchbacked, invalid boy in her hand on the very first day; and then he had simply grown, had learned to speak and to walk, to write and to read, had learned his craft, and in the end he had become her master. Especially now that his mother had died. Since then he spoke to her directly, giving orders (before he had always expressed them as childlike wishes): he wanted it this way or that way, at this time or that. She was the servant, but she had secretly also become a sort of mother to him. She unconsciously took on the tone and the manner of thinking of his late, real mother. And her manner of dress as well, up to a point. The photograph showed that clearly enough. And she did all this not to become the mistress of the house, but rather to remain a servant. The longer I waited there beside her, the better I liked her. I sensed the clean atmosphere of her kitchen and her chambers. God could come to her at any time. She wouldn't even have to dust off her wooden suitcase for him. In any event, cleanliness and subservience were a part of her religion. And these two traits had also saved her from the humiliations of old age. They would keep her in good hands in this life, until the day she died. I had noticed that, and she felt that I had noticed. And since I had discovered this before she did, in just a quarter of an hour, I had become more acceptable to her, and she looked at me a bit more mildly. I stared straight ahead. I was trying to find a reason to leave. All at once I didn't want to wait for the violin maker anymore; instead I wanted to secure a seat for myself at the circus, like Mr. Jakob.

I heard children's shouts, calling people together. I looked out at the street. An elephant was really going by. It seemed to me as if the street were growing older as this gray mountain moved through it. And once again the world was just a small, poor theater, a tiny circus for this enormous animal. It brought a tension into the city, so that people weren't content to stay within their own four walls. And other people must have felt the same way, because as I could see and hear, everyone was now out in the street. I caught wind of a carousel song. I was infected with carnival fever. I had to go out. I looked up again at the violins. I unconsciously gestured to one among those many, it was my own. It had made itself known to me again. I almost smiled. I wanted to take it down right away. But the maid, who seemed to know everything, said that it hadn't been broken in yet, maybe she knew because of where it was hanging. I would leave that to him if he thought that was needed. So I left. I was down in the street before it struck me. In my mind those small living quarters now seemed to fall in on themselves like a castle built of sandstone blocks, when a child shakes it. All it would take was a single event from this outside world, the kind that had been carefully avoided until now, and that life would be extinguished; the hunchback's life. I could really feel that, in my own flesh. Already my blood was beginning to flow along this great circuitous course. And I took things up in my small, hot hands, feeling them like those animals that we believe have no eyes. What if a dancer were to come between those peculiar fingers? She would recoil in horror, even at the thought.

For love was a matter of little interest to that man. God had kindly granted him these wonderfully clean rooms in which to make his home, and a maid and a mother, and all the violins of heaven. With all that, one could just as well do without love. I grew so agitated, and turned so strongly against that man. I even thought the birds were being too imprudent. With young girls' souls imprisoned in their bodies. In that moment I wouldn't have put so much as a mirror in his room. And yet things could have been quite different. He might have been superior to us, to the whole world. Something might happen that none of us had ever imagined.

"My God," I suddenly said; I had already arrived at the open square where the circus would take place, "what if by some terrific accident I end up sitting next to him!" I calculated. It was certainly possible. The inexpensive seats were long gone, and the wealthier parties would take their sweet time, and some wouldn't buy their tickets until evening. By now it even seemed to be a sure thing. After all, it was such a small city. When it came to important things, you were always everyone's neighbor. A child came toward me with a carnival hat on his head. A man came out from inside, selling little flags. I bought my ticket. I would have preferred to spend the afternoon there until the performance began. It seemed unnatural to return home again. But the world is so terribly big and wide and unwelcoming when we come there as strangers, tired and bored, seeking a place to sit. There is a meadow everywhere, but this is only for the poor little spectators who are so close to the ground to begin with, who have already been there for hours, not wanting to miss a single glimpse of what they have paid their pennies for. They have been living there for months, any time they had a free hour. But I, particularly as an adult, have no right to enter there. The poor have their own kingdom, too, and their own laws.

And on the southward side, where I finally found a little bench placed at the edge of the tent, a wind was blowing that was strong enough to numb you. And there was not a soul to be seen. There was just a paper kite that had broken loose and was flying off into the sky, observed by me alone, and no one else. It was a circus of wind that whipped the kite along, a stranger to itself and to the clouds. It was a fantastical drama. I was almost afraid. Solitude may be the only thing that can chasten a man who lacks humility, and bring him back to himself. It widens the space around him, lifts the heavens up like a gigantic banner, and lowers the earth beneath him. And he must live on it—this earth—after it has suddenly taken on the dimensions of the endless universe, has grown at once flat and round again. The earth is a giant, it is a globe on which we are not even a single point.

I had gotten so far away; I pulled myself up short like a dog and followed the scent of the world from which I had come. And we need only seek, and we will find it again. That is how animals, too, can find their way back to their previous masters—though the route may seem impossible.

But I would have had to become a beggar woman, or an orange vendor (I was too old to become a circus rider or an acrobat, let alone a poor child who slips under the wall of the tent, it was much too late for that), just to spend a few hours undisturbed beneath that circus canopy in the meadow.

So we weren't free to walk about where we pleased. Those who belonged at home had to go home. That was a proper rebuke for me; and so I only meekly returned to take my seat shortly before the performance began.

I was seated a bit below the middle. There were so many heads there, looking on, that at first it all confused me.

A child in a pink ballet dress on a horse! Now and then you could hear an imitative call cross her lips, and you noticed how silent it was in the circus. The music closely followed the child's lead, seeming to go on tiptoe. But then, as the child left the ring alongside her little horse, like a porcelain figure, the crowd found its voice again, first one and then another. And among those applauding people I recognized a woman who lived in my apartment house. And diagonally in front of me, it couldn't have been better, was the little hunchback. He sat motionless beneath his cape.

The music didn't leave us much time for reflection. A greyhound entered the ring. He shot through a paper hoop. His silver hair shimmered, seemingly wet from the speed. He could run through the legs of six wonderfully trained white horses. He wound around in a circle from one to the next like a wreath of flowers. Then suddenly he stood in the middle and took a bow by bending his head backwards. This dog was exquisitely suited to that sort of performance, in which everything depends on beauty. But in the first moment that he was free, he yawned as if unspeakably bored; and he seemed to leap into the jaws of the little lump of sugar that awaited him as a reward for his performance. And finally he disappeared. We were freed, and yet we regretted it. I was already so happy that I had forgotten any ulterior motive for my visit to the circus. (But even so I had not stopped reproaching myself for a single minute.)

How could anyone want to observe a person, to learn about

his nature … Laughter awakened me from this contemplation. Now the horses were alone. They were walking in a line. I looked around. Because I knew that couldn't be the cause of their laughter. It must have another meaning. Yes, indeed. A little hunchback was running along behind this train of holy white horses. He seemed to be tied to their shining pink tails. And now he was flying, simply by letting his legs go.

The whole circus was laughing, laughing with pipes and drums. The musical accompaniment was made for the occasion. Fear was coursing through my limbs. Yes, here they were, these people. And here was the circus in them. The whips cracked, one after another, invisibly in the air.

In my fear, I looked over in spite of myself to the little hunchbacked spectator. He was wrapped even smaller in his coat, and he wasn't moving. If someone had jostled him right now, even by accident, it probably would have created a scene; one of those agonizing spectacles that the world refuses to answer for. But the little hunchback in the circus ring was still swinging, and in the end he became like a ring himself, like an orbit. He became a ring that he himself had crafted, he merged with his own orbit, until finally he disappeared entirely beneath the sound of kettle drums and the whirl of snares and laughter. You couldn't say anything now, not even to yourself, the shouts drowned you out. And you had to stop for a moment in the midst of this watching; having lost your connection to the place where you were sitting. You were tired and wanted to sleep.

But then suddenly he was standing again, the clown, as if resurrected; on the backs of all the horses. He was screaming at them with a single fury. He wanted them to swim now, to drown in the grass that was surging like a flood. Light fell on him from somewhere, the rapidly changing flashes of fireworks. He looked so much like his brother in suffering, up there in the stands, that you could have mistaken one for the other. The circus had caught hold of them both. The latter man must have taken off his coat long ago, for he sat there unmasked before the world. How horrible the world can be. And even to itself. But perhaps this is its health, its only source of courage. By giving voice to everything, perhaps it finds itself again. Nevertheless, the violin maker's staid Sunday suit was only decorated with a watch chain and a few dangling silver thalers, it was nothing compared to the clown's finery. And those around him could hardly have noticed the resemblance. For the clown had a silky red shock of hair that stood up on top and stuck out to the left and right. And the face with its make-up looked out sadly from beneath the pointy white felt hat. He had little stars on his cheeks and chin and a half moon on his forehead. All of this made him larger and smaller, and seemed in some secret way to belong on his face. But then there was the many-layered lace collar that completely encircled this neckless man, repeating the circle of the dogs, the circle of the horses, and the circle in which he himself had flown. And after that came the giant hump that made this large man small, that folded him together as if to set him aside. This hump was the circus. It was the leap that everyone had to take here in the circus. First the animals, then the acrobats, tightrope walkers, and horse trainers; and then we ourselves, the spectators in the stands. But finally even those who had never gone to the circus, the whole rest of the world. In a sense, everyone at one time or another had hung from the tail of flying horses.

I sat there for a long time. But even in retrospect, I feel unable to describe the events that followed—.

After many madcap stunts and tricks, it was like a church procession when the twenty elephants left the ring. There was no need for music anymore. The people left.

And only when the tents had been taken down, and there was nothing left in the town that recalled the circus, did I go to my violin maker again to pick up the violin. I went there as if there had never been tents in the distance, I only wanted to feel what was there in the present again: the violin maker's room. It was nothing but a quiet Sunday that prompted me to go. The threat that lurked there was forgotten. And yet I might very well have still been thinking of it. In fact, it would have been quite possible. And in that case, wouldn't the whole episode have had to start again from the beginning? But I only fetched my violin, and inside everything was silent, as if no one was there. You could hardly say a word. In that silence, soft as velvet, everything was suspended. Even the hunchback himself was quiet, as if otherwise he might disturb someone. Only the stroke of the clock was there again, with its gentle reverberations. It was just three o'clock. I was on the verge of leaving, lost in thought as always happens there, when I caught sight of the mirror in the dark shadows:

A little picture was mounted below it, newly acquired. A hunchback stood there, a clown. He was taking a bow, with one hand propped on his side while the other held his hat as politely as could be, bidding farewell to anyone who still had something to ask.—

Susanna

We children were playing ourselves weary by the open window. The day had not yet faded, but for us it was an hour of rest.

My sister was speaking loudly.

Then a girl came into the room. Her hair was brown and hung down in long braids. Her dress gray, her skirt gray. We had to stop talking; this new girl looked so wise. "I heard that there are children in the house, may I play with you?"

We played, and when the clock struck eight, she took her knitting again and went back to her apartment.

Just then our mother came home, and we told her: "Susanna was here."

Countless times in those years I sat alone with my doll by the wall of the house that faced the garden, dreaming my way down those trellised paths.

Once, when I found our door locked, I went to the upstairs apartment.

Susanna was there. She was standing at the kitchen window, erasing something from a drawing.

Her mother was slicing bread for a long table, each piece in its proper place.

That sight of her would stay with me forever: large and

haggard, a dark countenance, her clothing all one color, black. She kindly offered me a piece of bread for my afternoon snack. Then I left again.

The next time I visited, it was already close to Christmas. A lamp cast its green light on the table. The family sat around it. The mother was knitting, the brothers were drawing. Others were flipping through illustrated magazines.

I didn't see the father anywhere. So I made straight for the oldest brother and begged him in a whisper: "Make my doll better, her head fell off." And there were a few little pictures on the music table, he gave them to me and pasted them onto the first page of an album. They always spoke in a whisper. They rarely had anything to say to each other. It never occurred to me to make noise, either. Just once I laughed, and the floor creaked under my foot. Then the man at the head of the table stood and leaned his white hair in my direction and roared: "Quiet!"

All these thoughts had been wiped away again by the time my mother said: "You can go up there again; Susanna's there."

I looked up into the air, asking questions in my mind.

"She had scarlet fever, she's in bed."

There was a room with two beds. Susanna was lying toward the window. Her eyes and her long brown hair were just like before. But her cheeks were pale.

Day after day I sat by her bed, and we chatted just as we had before. Her brothers and sisters, too, took turns sitting in her room, or sometimes neighbor girls visited to provide some entertainment.

And often, when the room was filled again with that old peaceful silence, I would pull a little gift from my pocket, one of my own prized possessions that my mother had put there as a present for her.

"But don't you want it yourself?" Susanna would always ask before reaching out her hand. But the joy that I felt for her was so evident that we owned everything in common.

When I entered the living room another time, I found her sitting there in the corner of her sofa. "She's visibly improving," her mother told me. But to me Susanna seemed quiet and a little sad. After a time, her sisters led her back to her room. She walked like an old woman, and her shape had changed as well. That alone was enough to tell me that she wasn't happy. When she was finally resting on her cushions, they told her about a wheelchair that they wanted to buy her to use during her recovery.

The doctors came. Two tall, dark men, and I thought that the man with the white hair must have done this to her.

I went down and played "Mother Hulda" by the little fountain in front of the garden. Weeks passed before I went up again to visit "Susi," as they called my playmate.

Early one spring morning her brothers and sisters called me again. Susanna was sitting upright in bed, her cheeks a ruddy brown, fiddling with colorful swatches of fabric and singing. We were all so happy. The sun was not yet burning, but it shone into our souls.

Then a girl from the neighborhood entered the room. She brought a doll with delicate limbs and a little knit jacket and hat and other nicely sewn doll clothes, as if it were a gift. But it wasn't. She pushed me away from the bed and played with the doll for Susanna to see. She made me angry with her skill and her eagerness. I always had to think about her red hair.

She turned toward the early morning sun and said: "Susanna, tomorrow's your birthday! Aren't you going to celebrate?"

Susanna was silent. But her mother smiled in from the

living room, and from that we could tell that there was a pleasant surprise in store for us.

The neighbor girl, satisfied, gathered up her doll things in her arm and left.

After that, the mother sat down next to Susi on her bed and talked to her about the coming day.

"Of course we'll leave the doors open for you."

The day passed, and the morning came, as beautiful as the one before.

There were buttercups and forget-me-nots on the bureau, and all sorts of gifts. Susanna's brothers had gathered the flowers for the bouquet very early, far from the city, and the table of gifts had been prepared with secret excitement before Susanna opened her eyes. They made her bed in festive white, and braided red ribbons into her hair.

In her hands she held a book of fairy tales that she always loved to read. Everyone was quiet. They all had jobs to do.

And so the afternoon arrived, and her thirteen guests sat around her in their festive dresses and white skirts, chatting. They told stories from school, and played forfeits, and then feasted in their cloudless gaiety.

We didn't even think about the fact that Susanna was sick. The children brought in chairs and played a wild circle game to the sound of a march.

As they were gently being herded from the room, the big old father came home with a sizable package under his arm. "Susi, guess what's in here," he said to her. "It's not for me, is it?" Susanna asked uncertainly, before she could think of anything. He pulled out a big doll with blonde hair and a blue necklace and a richly decorated little shirt.

Then he went back into his study. Just after that, the children all bid her farewell, and everyone wished her good health once again.

Susanna held the doll weakly in her hands. She reluctantly wrapped it up again and laid it at the end of her bed.

Then she held out her hand to me—to tell me that I should go, or should be quiet, or that I shouldn't think about it. But the doll was looking at me coldly through the wooden wall of its box, and I didn't move from my spot while Susanna fell asleep, sweating and moaning.

"Susanna has to die." We knew that, she and I, because of the doll.

Someone quickly turned down the bedspread, changed the sheets, and helped Susi return to her peaceful sleep. But the doll fell and shattered.

My mother called me to dinner. As I unexpectedly opened my eyes in the dark of night, it seemed to me that someone was crying above me, in my Susi's room.

The next morning, very early, I was with her again. With a mute sound she gestured to an oil lamp; she wanted it moved away from her. That was easy to understand. But she had no language anymore. It was even more silent up there now than it had been before, so that Susanna wouldn't have to think about the fact that she was mute.

She lost her hearing. She lost control of her limbs. And her eyes dimmed.

Her father walked through the room, hunched to death.

I wanted to forget everything, and I sat with my toys as I had before, by the wall of the house that faced the garden.

Then our maid came to me with tears in her eyes and said: "Susi is dead." Now I knew, and I went out to the street to wait for my mother.

She was in the middle of a cheerful conversation with a lady, but I interrupted her and said: "Mother, Susi is dead."

Her shock was enough for me. She rushed home, and the lady thoughtfully turned away. She looked up to the closed shutters.

But my pain was not yet allayed.

The brothers and sisters were standing at the other gate. I told them, too. They threw their school books on the ground and rushed into the house. And my sister Helene came. "Hey, I've told all the children. Susi is dead." She turned pale, and then said in a comforting tone, "We don't say dead, we say she passed away."

Then she walked through the streets with me, talking about other things. She was like me, her soul in disarray.

They were all strangers to me now, the people in the house. I stood at the window in the stairwell, watching the mourners come and go, and the wreaths. And the sympathy cards that fell into the box; all these things that felt so far from my heart.

Her mother came out, large and dressed in black, and asked me in tears: "Do you want to see Susi again?"

She was lying in the coffin. I knew that. I trembled and ran down to the garden.

My doll was lying by the wall of the house. Susi had always been so cheerful. I thought of her.

Then a line of schoolgirls, dressed in black, came around the corner. Following a wagon.

"Susanna is in heaven now.

"But Helene will be gone until evening, too, the cemetery is so far. The bells are ringing."

The Girl

A stroll through unknown territories, past small, unfamiliar properties, is not just a matter of walking, observing, and moving on. Somewhere those small, polished windowpanes, which always have the same lovely, well-tended fuchsias behind them, or the entrance hall of a house with its fresh-cleaned fragrance, or perhaps a white bench in front of the house, will imprint itself on our lives like a fine, archaic script.

Of course not all of them are like that. Some are in a state of slow decay. But for each person who seems to have fallen asleep on his estate, another is waiting to renovate it and bring it back into shape. As his own property, mind you, but what does that mean, except for that age-old and ever-present truth: that nature has made a pact with the mighty of this earth. These are all binding bills of sale: nature gives its grain, its trees, its furs, in short, it gives everything, everything it has. But man, for his part, cannot simply hold out his hands for a while. He must give his flesh and blood for ownership, indeed, he must give something which, at times, he takes nature herself to be lacking; he must give his own soul.

Yet sometimes nature, too, can be content with a lease. But

all too often the tenants are poor, downtrodden people. They work up to deadlines, and appear and disappear again like shadows.

And in the country everyone can tell, even at three paces, if someone is an owner or a tenant. They can tell at least that much, if not much more. But this only makes a poor man doubly poor. For he is poor not only to himself, but to others as well.

All the more so if he is not just poor. If he has fully gone to seed. If he can no longer even offer to perform useful work for others. If poverty has shown itself in him, has made him a beggar to it, so that just as another man puts all his work into assembling a witty carnival costume, this man becomes an ever more consummate image of poverty. And in the end he is a consummate beggar, but the stages that he passes through on the way are very gradual, and barely visible to an observer. But sometimes (for it often happens in the end that hares, half-starved and fleeing for their lives, are pecked to death by birds, and so life reaches a great and seemingly unjust conclusion), sometimes everything takes a different turn, as if the story to be told were nothing but a peaceful idyll, an idyll of poor people, almost like those icons of saints in which the very slightest thing can touch our hearts, can touch our hearts more, in fact, than the most precious gifts of the three kings. But these poor people can hardly make it anymore, at least not on their own. They must be guided back into their own lives, so to speak. They have become too accustomed to sitting before the door of their own heart. And so it is nature's duty to find someone who will show them to their own beds, who will give them their own bread to eat again, will give them a simple sip of water to show that they can recover their strength. But of course this providence does not amount to mercy as we understand it; since it is all-knowing, and because it follows the paths that are there to be taken, this providence often begins by putting those poor people up for sale, the very people it intends to help, putting them in a position that is simply laughable. For it really is a funny thing when such a good-for-nothing ends up at one of the many out-of-the-way auctions of this world.

"He," or in this case let's say "she," it normally amounts to the same thing, need only stop to rest a bit from walking beside a country road, and already the buyers are passing. "Hm," thinks a farmer boy, healthy, heartlessly healthy, appraising only with his eyes this ware that could be had at a modest price, marked down, so to speak: "so, she's missed her chance, too." And he goes on his way, whistling. Then a young lady with a gentleman, tourists, very curious: people whose house is so well-kept, so rich and impregnable, that they see a pleasing landscape as nothing more than the extension and surroundings of that house, and they react with surprise, as they would in a park, when suddenly they come upon a stranger taking a rest, wondering where he possibly could have come from. What's more, I would even say that with their curiosity, they unconsciously seek to drive this poor person away. There is something there that cannot be resolved: "What could have happened?" they think; she's wearing a dress much like our own, though it may be weathered and of a different cut, still from a distance it seems equally proper. "She looks legitimate, yes, she looks like one of our own class. But her child never will be." And they're right, they've judged it all with a single look. Then along comes a farmer woman, one who rarely speaks. She has her own firm rules. She has grown into the world and become its center, if only at a single spot, for we generally cannot be in several places at once. She would never sit down beside this woman. She has just sold her surplus of flax in the little market town, with its cloister tower and a street of houses peeking out over the wall. Even the richest farmer's daughter doesn't need more than fifty pairs of stockings for her dowry, the old farmer's wife says to herself as she continues on her way, and flax stockings can be rough for someone who hasn't grown up with them. She looks thoughtful, she seems to have something in the corners of her mouth. Maybe she's thinking about more than just flax stockings. Then some children come along. They look. They stand there, and, as they consider this riddle, they become a riddle themselves. Time passes. The person there on the bench would start to see herself as a scarecrow of curiosity (but there's nothing to be done about that) if something didn't happen soon. Her hat is a white straw hat, an innocent shape, with no decoration to speak of. Two little leaves hang from the metal band, and a single lily of the valley. The skirt is of two colors, brown in the front and moss green in the back, decorated all around with a pattern left by lace that has long since been removed. The sun will have its little fun, just as people do. Then along comes the messenger who serves these mountains. And although he is always on his way somewhere, resting on one leg while moving forward with the other, as he says himself, nevertheless he stops there, still hunched over, but peering out to see whatever can still be seen with his old eyes. The person there is young, and actually she's almost pretty. She would be truly pretty if fortune had been kinder to her. But "good fortune," he knows, "is not an accident, it's a genuine character trait." This gives him a moment's pause. But then, after just a short conversation, he makes the right move. He takes her on. "Come along," he says, "you can feed yourself and your child at my house all right." (She doesn't have a child yet, but he could still be right.) "Can you cook?" "Not much." "Doesn't matter. Can you sew?" "Not really." "Doesn't matter. Can you milk goats?" "Not at all." "Doesn't matter either. And you don't garden?" She shakes her head. "That's all right too," he says with understanding or sympathy. "Once you live with me, you'll learn. When you have a child, you'll learn. I'll show you how to do the work, you just haven't learned yet, mostly, so I'll tell you what to do." An old man from the Odyssey couldn't have had a clearer view of life.

And as the shadow fell across the hills and mountains, extinguishing the light of the air, this girl's life, too, had changed, and she was busy at work in a little house, even if she was also timid, as was her nature. And the bench was dark and empty. It could lean on itself for all I care. Or the night could take hold of it. Maybe there was already another apprentice sleeping on it, or a pair of lovers meeting. Once such a summer night has fallen dark, and all who don't fully belong there have gone, it grows transparent again. Then perhaps the flowers dream that they are stars. And perhaps they truly believe it, for in the morning they awaken with their hearts crusted in diamonds. And the birds' throats are never as fresh as after a clear, balmy, starlit night.

A single night, if there were only one on earth, would have to be left at peace, and allowed to pass this way. Even the sternest townsman would surely agree. But the day, too, is just like this sky, this heaven of trembling worlds. And so we have no need for night, says this man of the town. In the morning we believe that we can see to the other end of the world. In any case, light is as valuable as gold as we go about our work. It takes us in hand as if we were a washbasin, filled early in the morning, and as if we were a fire, promptly lighted. And as if we were the first food of the day, earnestly relished. But then it is time to work, as if we have made a covenant with God. And we would have to be very weak and poor in conscience if we were to break this covenant and go on our way and sit around here and there and finally nod off in the midst of a bell-bright day. Because it's true, this light is ringing; it rings until it sets, and our continent turns away to face the night.

It's hard to believe how quickly everything goes when we believe in the work and in ourselves. It seems bewitched, in a positive sense. Of course, when the old man pulled on the jacket that the girl had mended for him, it wasn't mended as a nun would have done it, or even any other woman. But it was mended all the same. And it was somehow touching that it was done at all. It was like listening to a child just learning to read. This work, likewise, was still slow and uncertain. But it was coming, and that was the main thing, after all. And over time, because some of the work was the same each day, she gained practice. The reaping went a little better. The nanny goat stood still to be milked. So the pail grew full, and as the days passed there were signs that she was doing something right. And hadn't she taken to cooking much more naturally than anyone could have expected? And when she'd done her day's work well, didn't the old man treat it with respect, like a bridegroom? And she had done it well! Soon she could do all of her chores. He had judged rightly at first sight. And she was more content than anyone could be. He had chosen a good one. She had needed a place like this for a long time, an isolated little house with two goats and nine hens, with a garden on all sides and a meadow. This grandfatherly old man must have been created for her before time began, and so as often as she saw him, she always treated him like a work of providence. And that's no bad way to treat a person. On the contrary, it's a heavenly way. If that could last forever, people would feel eternity around them. An eternity, even if we measure it by the stars and not in God's terms, is still a considerable stretch of time, long enough to begin and conclude many a thing.

And so it's no surprise that in relatively few months this practice turned to skill, skill to cleanliness, order, and in short, constancy, so that the old man would have taken up his messenger routes again, had he not already begun to concern himself like a grandfather with the young lady's approaching delivery. "You know," he said one day, "I'll tell the midwife. Then you'll be taken care of." And even as he said that, he was already standing at the door in his large curved hat, his vest, and his long coat, already reaching out with his hand and his tall walking stick toward the road that led through the forest. "Yes," he said, already on his way, since like most old people he didn't listen to others, but simply spoke into the shapeless world of his soul. For the soul has already begun its journey with Father Charon, even as the man lives on for months and years in his house, going his own way and doing as he pleases, as people do.

Now the woman was alone.

She was called Julia, and sometimes other things as well. It had turned out that she still had a wooden suitcase filled with clothes, and even a small sum in the bank, one day the postman had brought her the interest. But it made no impression on her. Things lay where they lay, and that one green dress seemed to have grown stuck to her body. But now, hardly had the old man disappeared when a strange eagerness overtook her. She cut up a shirt, following a paper pattern that she had trimmed to size—(she couldn't even really quite imagine just how big a newborn child was).—Then she took a very soft bed sheet and hemmed its edges to make diapers. In between, she reaped, she milked, she weeded the garden, and she made the soup for supper. But when the old man came home, there was already an armful of children's clothing there, finished and unfinished. And he looked on this accomplishment with satisfaction, for somehow he knew that it was an achievement for her, and he was pleased that she had taken his hint. She had now been brought into the order of the world, and the old man, if he hadn't been so old, would have had to free her from it again. For he had enough insight to understand that such a thing was required in order for this wounded soul to be fully reconciled, even if he was not the man to do it. He understood that. For this creature still spoke no more than those few words that came naturally. And this troubled him, for she was young and must have wanted to speak. But she wasn't sad, either. On the contrary: she gave her consent in advance to everyone and to everything that happened. But there was something that she lacked, something that is part of human life in general, even if it is not a noble quality: a certain and ungrateful joyfulness; that was what she lacked. Yes, she even said so herself. She was lacking something.

It was as if a soul only inhabited this body by chance. And each lived separately, for itself. And that was why it took so long to bring her actions into accord with her nature, and that was why it was surely no mere coincidence that she had met this ancient but hearty messenger, who became her master.

One evening the old man went out again on the country road. But he had already summoned a neighbor, a woman with ten children. She was milking now, and preparing the coffee, real coffee, and there was also a tall copper pail full of water over the fire; most likely the bath for the child that was to come … She looked at the little clothes. Oh God, the little shirt was much too small! The girl was still so lacking in common sense, though she would soon become a mother. But fortunately the farmer's wife didn't know that the girl had sewn it herself. And besides, this poor farm wife, too, had been well schooled by fate, so that even if she had known the truth, it would only have caused her a bit of pain, or incomprehension. Indeed, she would simply have sacrificed some of her own children's clothing, as hard as this would have been for her; even if (as was in fact the case) it were only a trade. Indeed, even if (as was also the case) she had failed, as always, to keep this story to herself, and had gossiped about it in the village, and even shown everyone the tiny shirt, inhumanly small: still it would have been a good deed, and still the girl would have repaid this act of kindness.

For keeping silent is too great a task for many people, it's too much to ask of every third person. And comprehension, to begin with, is only the palate of our understanding, but the palate is connected to the tongue. And the tongue—ordinarily— (once it has understood): speaks. This is the way of the world.

But as I've said, it's already quite a feat when the tongue is no longer simply the tongue, or the understanding, when instead it transforms itself again into heart and hand. And so the girl had cause to rejoice when the farmer woman came by with three little smocks and two shirts. For there was poverty on both sides, if not the same poverty. And the farmer woman felt secure by comparison to her sister in suffering. But the latter, as she slowly began to feel the terrifying travails of childbirth, felt a sort of horror at this mother of ten children. Nature tore this creature into four parts, if only in her pained imagination. Julia, I must resolve to call her by name again, gripped the edges of the straw bed with her hands, her outermost ends. Her feet were stretched out like a dead woman's. Her head was turned back, as if it were no longer a part of her body. But now and then she went limp again and lay there like a weary animal dropping off to sleep. And in this, nature does not distinguish between a princess and a beggar woman. And if the princess demands a narcotic, it seems to me that this makes her more perishable than a plant, which, in its metamorphosis, breaks the capsule of its bud with its own strength, its final burst of living and dying. It is no coincidence that the landscape of the earth is identical to that of the heart. Outside, as the first snow fell, coming late this year, it quickly melted again and ran in many rivulets down the street. It was night, but like that summer night, the day of a night. But somewhat bleaker, befitting the season. You could forget to look up at the stars, because they appeared not only far away, but also very small. Inside the room everything seemed paralyzed, for as soon as other people make use of our belongings before our eyes (and all the more so when they wish to help us), those objects fall dead, and against our will we think of how it shall be here when we ourselves have died.

The door of the cottage opened. The midwife was there, and she set down her things. And the old messenger, who was satisfied now and had intended to go to his bedroom, remained standing, as if rooted in the open doorway. It was as if he needed to go out to the road again, to stay outside, to wander outside forever. And it was already night, with the stars in their dazzling splendor, detached from the world down below. Oh, how alone we can be. There was a cry. But not a cry of pain, rather, it was the sound of something splitting apart, and a child's cry entered the world. It ruled over this world for a moment like a flash of lightning. Thinking and feeling are no longer just thinking and feeling. And even if there was only a single small lamp burning there, now the black of the darkness itself—as peculiar as it may sound—boldly came to light. It was not clear if this was death or life. The old man sat broken on the edge of his bed, while in the living room someone spoke and someone answered. It must have been the midwife and the farmer's wife. But after a while there were four and then five voices, the mother and the child had joined the conversation. As if they had both been born.

With that, old Joe found his feet again. He stood again. And finally the midwife called to him from the next room, teasing: "Joey, you've got a granddaughter." And the meaning of these words seemed to make this life a place to live again. The table in the middle of the room held the light, the tiny lamp, bearing it up in a touching gesture, offering it to all the objects in the room. The small beam that fell on the bench lit its clean cloth cover. Two pictures could be distinguished on the wall, illustrations from books. And a Jesus on the wall, only silver now, spread through the room like a holy spider web. You could have sunk to your knees. There are moments when we need not be ashamed of anyone, when it is Christmas in the soul. But with birth we have the crucifixion and the resurrection, and we can only be thankful; we can no longer say if it was someone else's anguish or our own that we have suffered. Old Joe didn't trust himself to look over to his maid's bed right away. Although of course he knew: she was lying there with her child.

Oh, what a redemption that was. After all of that distress and fear, there was no choice but to love this child. It would cry for you, and by comforting it, you comforted yourself. Only slowly did he follow her voice, and he gently stroked her while still standing, as if from afar. He lifted the head of the fiery red little creature and dangled some of his own white hair in front of her. That was meant as a joke, or a sort of greeting. He marveled at the powerful little hand that blindly held fast to whatever it was given to grab, and he felt that he could hardly free himself again. And soon a new bond was formed, between an ancient man and a newborn child. And finally the midwife and the farmer's wife could go in peace, because the old man was joyfully prepared to perform all the necessary tasks. He kept vigil at night, you could say. As he sat there on his careful watch, he almost resembled one of the three kings. For certainly he knew, too, that this child brought his household into being. Earlier he had wondered at times how long his young housekeeper would last. But now he knew that she would work for the child's sake. And this was a different sort of work. And only this work could become what work should be: the two chain links of life. So he listened to be sure that both were breathing, mother and child. And if a stranger had reproached him, claiming that this was a calculating, loveless love, that would only have proven that the stranger understood nothing of life, for life consists of nothing but these relationships. They are its nature, its own life. The more noble a man is, the more strongly they are usually expressed in him. And it was like being woken from the dead when these relationships, which had died, were renewed. And life pulled the old man along in his new role. And the work that he had done by himself all those years, that he had half neglected, came to the fore again, and he worked for hours, hardly taking time to catch his breath. Even the spoons made his acquaintance again, and so, clumsily, did the bowls and plates. Guided by Julia's weak voice, he pulled out things that had long since dropped from his sight. What he had first undertaken as an act of charity, life now compelled him to continue. Indeed, he took a small child in his arms for the first time in his life, this small child. And that amazed him above all. This creature slept and slept. She slept from the exhaustion of being born, or perhaps because there, in the blanketing warmth of the farmer's house, she felt as if she were in her mother's womb again, she slept almost without interruption, day and night. And because she didn't eat for thirty-six hours, she remained pure, almost a symbol of holy poverty. The little white handkerchiefs that passed for her clothes hung over the stove: drops of sweat beaded on the little windowpanes and ran down one after another. The clock struck. A hen, unaccustomed to silence, flew in through one of the adjacent rooms. Fourteen days passed in this way.

A real love unfolded between mother and child. The child's love for the mother was still invisible, as if blind. But the mother's love for the child was so much like love itself that it appeared to embody it. But this, too, was a mistake. And therein lay the seed of her insubstantial being; that may be what sealed her fate. Nevertheless, she had made a covenant with a person for life, and that is the essential thing about the relationship between a mother and child. They both know, each time they see each other again: what we say and do to each other, it is forever. It will never fade. This is true even for parents and children who are strangers to each other due to certain turns of fate. This covenant simply cannot be destroyed, under any circumstances.

The farmer woman came for three weeks to work in the stall and in the house. For she saw at once that Julia couldn't be expected to get up on the third day and wash the diapers herself, the way a country woman would. And Julia slept, too, almost as much as the child. On the first day when she was well enough to stand, she was shocked to find that she had to learn to walk again.

The short walk to the bench by the stove felt like drowning. She didn't trust herself to lift the child for several days. The good old man kept taking care of everything. And so she owed him greater thanks than she had ever owed anyone in her life. Now this gratitude became her actual source of strength. It was also her only sort of happiness, she had no other. Life must have dealt her a brutal blow. Her childish nature could have been a sort of happiness. But it was always expressed in timidity, in her fear of every single unknown, unfamiliar movement. Even if one word was kind, if one action seemed clear and affirming, the next one, for reasons unknown, might be just the opposite. Oh life! How terrifying it was. It always seemed as if she herself had no mother, no husband, no brothers or sisters. As if life had just cast her out the door the day before. She still looked like that. Now she could do something, though, now she could do her work! And she had found a home for herself, too. And not just for herself. Her child was growing up alongside her. The child's name was Maria. And there was something temple-like about her, that offered instruction in life. From the beginning of her second year, she was strictly obedient, and uncompromising in her love of order. Her few building blocks were always kept together, and when she was called from her play, she never failed to come. It seemed that she unconsciously aspired to grasp those circumstances of life that her mother had never managed to reach for out of her own darkness. For even if Julia was well-meaning to a fault, still you couldn't deny that she was the sort of person others commonly refer to as "dumb." Oh, God knows what she was. But one thing was clear: she was lacking something.

And, what wonder, the old grandfather treated her accordingly. He treated her like a healthy invalid. But the child was his enchanted little bird, his little flower. In time the child replaced his daily walks, for he was growing more hunched over and weary. The destinations of his walks grew closer and closer. Fewer and fewer people entrusted their messages to him. The church in its sweet charity still sent him here and there, for he had always been loyal and reliable. But eventually he stopped taking any jobs. He wandered through his house, hunched to death. It was a wonder that someone could still live bent over like that. But for little Maria, he seemed just right. She never had to reach her arm up higher than it could go, the old man was always bending his head down to her. Indeed, soon he was walking beside her at the very same height, as mothers some- times do out of love. How wise this old man was. But he was not so unaware of himself as people might think. For often, when he encountered someone while going on his way (but he rarely ventured out anymore, for once, to his great dismay, he had suddenly found himself in an unfamiliar place, that is, he no longer knew where he was, since that seemingly small thing, memory, had let him down), for often, when he encountered someone, he simply stood still, looked up to that person, or to the sky, and gave a speech. And these were always truths that he spoke.

Once, since he was not entirely without practical concerns in this world, he told a visiting parish clerk that he wanted little Maria to be able to remain in the house, so after his death it should be sold to the mother at a modest price. "After all," he said with emphasis, "you can't take your money to heaven." And he thought to himself: "I can do what I want with my money." So he made a curious decision. He signed over his savings to the little one. But his savings were equal to the sale price of the house, so that Julia both bought her inheritance and received it as a gift. Surely this somehow reflected his feelings for her. When his decision became known, there was much talk of it in the village. Some people laughed, others didn't know what to think anymore. But in the house the day passed almost monotonously, like a day in the life of a tree, an unchanging day. The necessary things were done, one after the other, and already it seemed that nothing was changing anymore. Except that one human sun was slowly, slowly setting, and the child was growing into a person, and already the world in which she lived, in which she formed her thoughts, was in her eyes. She sat for half a day at a time beside the old grandfather, as if she felt that if she didn't now, soon she wouldn't be able to do so at all. And a young lamb that had almost died of loneliness came along, too, softly bleating to him in its melancholy. But the old man was almost like Abraham, who could no longer tell Isaac from Jacob, when the one creature stood to his right, the other to his left. Yet he could feel Juliette's strong arms, strengthened by the even strain of work, he felt those arms, and gladly allowed them to lead him back into his house.

One morning, oh, it was still early, he saw the spires of St. Mary's cathedral. And the road that led there was a high road, a road through the clouds. He followed this road with his words. Julia sat at the edge of his bed with tears in her eyes. She saw his spirit leave his body, and she was powerless to find even a single word to hold it back. Because we must know that death is always right.

She saw at once what she had dimly felt before, that now that he was gone, she was back on that bench beside the country road again, and people were passing by, sizing her up. But she sensed that Joe, the old man, was not among them this time, and that she had only learned these things now in order that she should suffer all the more. For just as nature forces a one-armed man to use his mouth and his right hand in place of the left, to use his whole body in place of this one missing hand, so that now, instead of just one hand, suddenly he is expected to have ten at any moment; just as it was for him, so it was for her as well. So it was for her as well: "Why didn't you properly train your soul, so that it could live within your body as a useful, functional thing; can't you hold yourself together? Don't you think someone could find a use for you? Oh, I can still use you as a scarecrow, if nothing else. Sure, you're good enough for that …" And tears ran down Julia's cheeks, unabating. Now she was lonely, in the worst of ways, as we are when someone has passed on. And the child brought in peppermint from the garden, as if she could sense her mother's powerlessness. The dying man came ever closer to his cathedral. He rang with his hands, as if imitating the bells. Finally the church took him in. And soon he looked just like that sarcophagus, stretched out long and covered over by the night of eternal sleep.

The child went away. But outside she picked flowers, and when she thought she had enough, she sat down on a rock, surrounded by her flowers and leaves, and waited as only children can wait. Evening came, dusk fell, the evening star rose over the house of this good shepherd of men, and the child fell asleep, and if Julia hadn't known that her child came to this spot, she would not have easily found her.

Candles stood in their candlesticks, and a Sunday sense of order filled every corner of the little house. The child slept by herself in the small adjacent room, and the next morning she ran in between unfamiliar people, hardly even recognizing her own home. A wake like that is a serious thing. We never forget it as long as we live. And that is good. Those who have not seen death up close are only halfway human, because death, too, is a part of life. First, fresh sheets were put on the bed, as if a new guest were coming, then water was fetched from the well, and vinegar, and a burial gown from the cabinet; stiff and dreadful in its way. Then the body was washed. Like the forest floor after heavy downpours, the veins lay exposed, and the bones were pushing out, rising up, as it were, to form the one image that persists in death. To a person like Julia, this most human of all things seemed the most inhuman; it required an immense effort for her to perform this duty. She was not lacking in love, she had tended his sickbed for years without a second thought, but this sight pushed her pain beyond its limits. And one must be fully drawn into this life, to be able to wash and clothe an old man like that for the grave. The farm girls took turns praying by the coffin, while the others stayed beneath the crucifix in the corner of the room, singing hymns. These sounds continued throughout the hours of day and night, until it was time for the body to be taken away. There was life in the house, but on tiptoes, with a lowered head. There were more people there than could fit into the house, and yet they didn't even fill the space. Everyone withdrew to his own spot as much as he could. And the ties that they had to one another were meant not for them, but for the dead man. They all offered Julia their hands. But even the day after the funeral they were less forthcoming with their greetings, and by the third day she had been forgotten. And it wasn't just that she was a stranger, or that they looked down on her on account of her child. No, in this region in particular, people lived in desperation, like iron glowing in the blacksmith's tongs, and no one had much time or inclination to speak or think of others. But no, it was because everyone felt that she was not human. If she had been in harmony with the world, or even only with herself, she would have enjoyed the friendship of the neighbors. But as things stood, what was alone within her was alone outside, as well.

Two older women came. They both received a stipend from the church, and they wanted to rent the room that now stood empty. They were not good souls. They had none of the old man's caring qualities. But Julia took them in. She had her own plan for them. She took them on as tenants, putting the house at their disposal, and keeping only a small profit in return. Then she tailored little skirts for the child—far from being too small, these skirts seemed meant to fit for several years to come—and she cleaned some things for herself.

How quickly poverty can be prepared to travel. Two little bundles, and the few Sunday clothes that are worn for the trip, and there's nothing left to be forgotten. It only takes a single glance to survey everything in the house, to see where it stands and how it stands. The flowers with their colorful eyes in their pitiful little beds in the garden are the only things that might try to hold one back. For who knows, when harshness and denial hold sway, if the flowers will not be the first target for hatred.

But there are some farewells that brook no opposition. After discussing a few details, and pointing out this and that, they left the house. Little Maria moved through the unfamiliar world as if she were made of glass, and her mother seemed to have nearly forgotten the little market town that she had walked through years before, and the bench where she had rested. It was spring again, the air seemed to race through the world with a joyful breath, like a frisky horse. It did not hurt the tall fir trees, it caused no pain to the little flowers or the poor people. On the contrary, everything was waking up. It was the right day for a resolution, it was the newly opened page of a book of legends that had yet to be written. Little Maria could easily walk in and disappear among the letters and their meanings. First they went into the church, where the silver bell that rang for mass could take its measure against the silver voice of this child. For she didn't know yet that the church is a quiet place. For Julia, this church was like an antechamber to the cloister where she planned to house her child for several years. She went out to a little door and rang for the prefect. Simple words are quickly understood. They were brief, just as their farewell had to be, a bit poorer now, for she had left behind what little money she still had. Everything happened so quickly, it was as if the little one had only looked around. And her mother was gone. And everything looked as if it were carved on an old wooden panel. There was the dormitory, and there was a school. And somewhere else there was a garden, and at another end was the refectory. And the church was everywhere, even in the dormitory. But no matter where she waited, her mother was nowhere to be found. But Maria was a child accustomed to her fate. She felt that her mother had done this herself, and so she didn't cry. Indeed, after a time she would not even have thought about her mother, she would have become a tiny nun. But the sisters consoled her, and in their minds they cried her unwept tears. She soon learned to read and write, learned the words of conversation and the words of prayer. And she learned to sing and to do needlework in linen, and to keep a room or a house in order and well fed. She would surely have become a lay sister, if the nuns had not made a special place for her mother in her thoughts. And since they taught her not to forget her mother, she did not forget. That was her nature. She had become a pillar of obedience and proper upbringing. She was a small miracle. Like a saint in a coffin. But despite this lifelessness, which she had also inherited, there was a power within her: she embodied the spirit of her golden background, the church. And she had to sense this in spite of her great innocence, otherwise she wouldn't have been the way she was. The prefect smiled each time she saw her, though she was otherwise a serious woman. And outside, her mother might not have been living as she should, she might have forgotten the little holy cross that God had bestowed upon her. Or she might not have known God, might never have given thanks to him, until the end of her life. But the nuns never spoke of that. Least of all to the child. And that was good. For what can we know. A soul's desperation is often a struggle with death. While we are far off, lost in speculation, the trunk tears itself out of the earth by its own roots. Ah God, such a poor person! For he doesn't die as soon as he is uprooted. He goes through the world bearing this mark, and he knows that he is not at home anywhere. Though he has committed no murder, still he is Cain.

Only one thing is certain: Julia went to one of the larger cities and visited old friends. But they were not the same. Her own lack of interest, and of love, had failed to sustain these ties in the face of distance and change. They talked past her, and she past them. And besides, Julia needed an income. And so she had to move on, to a place where there was one to be had. So she came to another small city. It was a time when everyone was seeking a new life, like a migration. But Julia was not so enterprising, she didn't go to America or to Jerusalem. A weaving mill was hiring untrained laborers. She took her place among them. And she stayed in this job for nearly ten years. She was so quiet and undemanding that they began to see her as one of their own. And it was precisely what she lacked that made her so well suited to a factory, for those places are practically made for such soulless or bodiless people—which is what she was, once and for all. And the fact that this woman never stole anything, or kept flawed wares for herself, which was halfway permitted, seemed like a miracle as well. And it was also a sort of relief that she never asked to be moved to the looms where patterns were woven with flowers and vines. She worked at the gray loom, once and for all. And she never took sides in a quarrel, or made any friends. But it wasn't as if she were sad, no, it would be more accurate to say that she was satisfied, in a primitive way. She had understood that she was not self-reliant, not independent in a certain sense. And if death had chosen to take her away from her little house and garden, then she just had to seek other accommodations. And since she couldn't hope to find such a good old friend just anywhere she looked—someone who would take not only her, but also her child, into his care and protection—she had to find her own place for the little one, too. This is how things were for her. And it was a miracle that she understood, and an even greater miracle that she acted accordingly. Of course no one disturbed her in this one harmony that she still had. But in her childhood and her early youth, even before she was born, in the restless existence of her forebears, she must have already been broken and brought low and crippled to the point of exhaustion. Wasn't it an angel that simply folded her hands in this way? And that called her at just the right time, like the fragrance of flowers, called her to follow blindly, with the simple experience of her failings?

Indeed, that urged her to provide for her future? For on her own she never would have managed—on her own she lacked all the energy that another person or an institution might have had for her. On her own she never would have succeeded in raising her child in that little farmhouse, without a master. She hardly would have understood the point of this upbringing;

for in her eyes, for her, life was basically empty and hollow. Indeed, it still seemed this way to her when she was with others, but then she bore it patiently, with friendly gratitude, like a precious gift that she really hadn't needed.

Of course this insight was not the insight of a single day, or of a single disappointed night of love, though even the most trivial incident from her childhood ought to have been enough to tell her who and what she was. But she had not learned this all at once. All the hours of her life, added together, had made it clear as day to her: You are clumsy to the point of foolishness, you are asleep in the deepest sense. You are without love, though you are patient and almost good. For I killed your love in the frost of spring. And a person cannot truly live without love. And yet I, nature, will not let you perish. You shall experience unto the end who you are and what you are, and who others are and what they are. And I will even grant and teach a few things to you. But even that will not enrich you in any true sense. All that will belong to you is poverty: all that you are denied, those intangible things that you never receive. This is my intention, to which you must be faithful. And this faith, if you will, shall be your only victory.

That was what her fate had decided for her. Unspeakably harsh and yet mild, denying and refusing and yet giving, indeed, casting all of this upon her. For such understanding is a great gift. Of course, as her thoughts wandered into the gray cloth she wove, they often turned to the single street of that small market town, and the bench, yes, the bench. And the old man and the house. But she wove without impatience, in the course of the slow growth of time itself, until the street finally became a street, the bench let her pass by unscathed, and her child's cloister waved to her from this pious embroidery. She had the good fortune that after these years had gone by, the two poor women who had rented her house grew old, and had to find new quarters elsewhere. So she could move in without any trouble. But first she rang the prefect's bell to claim her child. She knew this girl. It was just as she had imagined. The way that she stood there with her little suitcase, grown and yet still a child. But a pure, uncompromising child, whose weakness had been transformed into her strength. She had no need to bid a formal farewell to the prefect, for at the moment her departure was only a transition from one cloister to another. And there was no kiss for the reunited mother and daughter, in its place was a mutual reverence. A kiss is something that belongs at the end of life.